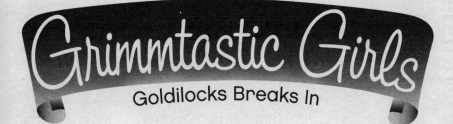

Grimmtastic Girls

Goldilocks Breaks In

Grimmtastic Girls

Grimmtastic Girls

Goldilocks Breaks In

Joan Holub & Suzanne Williams

Scholastic Inc.

ISBN 978-0-545-78394-1

Text copyright © 2015 by Joan Holub and Suzanne Williams
All rights reserved. Published by Scholastic Inc.
SCHOLASTIC and associated logos are trademarks and/or registered trademarks of Scholastic Inc.

12 11 10 9 8 7 6 5 4 3   16 17 18 19 20/0

Printed in the U.S.A.   40
First printing, May 2015

For our grimmighty Grimmtastic Girls readers:

Raven G., Lorelai M., Julia K., Maddy W. and Aijay W., Micci S.,
Haley G., Riley G., Renee G., Courtney C., Jasmine R.,
Megan D., Jaden B., Taelyne C., Caitlin R., Hannah R.,
the Andrade Family, Kristen S. and Erin K., Tessa and
Alexandria M., Jolee S., Jenna S. and Sarah S., Christine D-H.
and Khanya S., Cheyanne W., Alyson H., Serenity U. and
Destiny U., and you!

— J.H. and SW

Contents

It is written upon the wall of the great Grimmstone Library:

Something E.V.I.L. this way comes.
To protect all that is born of fairy tale, folktale, and nursery
rhyme magic, we have created the realm of Grimmlandia. In
the center of this realm, we have built two castles on opposite
ends of a Great Hall, which straddles the Once Upon River. And
this haven shall be forever known as Grimm Academy.

~The brothers Grimm

1

Locks and Keys

$\mathcal{I}$t was nearly midnight on Monday when Goldilocks went sneaking down the twisty stairs from her dorm room in Ruby Tower. She was on her way to find the magical Grimmstone Library. Since it constantly changed its location within Grimm Academy, you always had to hunt for it.

She searched the entire fourth floor of the Pink Castle, then took the grand staircase down to the third floor. There, Goldie quickly spotted the unmarked doorknob — the one without the GA logo that stood for Grimm Academy. It was on the wall right next to Ms. Blue Fairygodmother's Bespellings and Enchantments classroom.

"There you are!" she murmured gleefully. She reached out and gave the knob a twist.

Honk! It immediately morphed into a goose head. Perhaps because the hour was so late, it was wearing a nightcap — a polka-dot one with a long pointy top that had a fluffy ball at the end of it.

Goldie couldn't help giggling. "That cap of yours is hilarious!" she told the gooseknob.

"Well, how rude of you to say so!" the knob replied, all in a snit. "It gets cold in these halls at night, you know. Ask any metal doorknob about that." Its eyes lowered to the floor. "And at least I'm not wearing ginormous furry slippers."

Goldie glanced down at her feet, surprised to see that she was wearing her big fluffy bear-head slippers. She'd worn her dress to bed tonight on purpose, but her feet had gotten cold, so she'd put on these slippers, too. Once the alarm she'd set had gone off, she'd hopped out of bed and been in such a rush to sneak down here and locate the library that she'd forgotten to change to regular shoes.

Argh! She hoped she didn't run into any teachers out here in the halls. Not only would she get in trouble for breaking curfew, she'd also be horribly grimmbarrassed to be caught in these childish-looking slippers. Although she was petite and did look a little younger than most students her age, she was twelve years old — not two!

"Sorry," she told the gooseknob. "I can't help it. I say what I think."

The knob wasn't soothed. "A habit that doesn't win you a lot of friends, I imagine," it replied tartly.

Too true, thought Goldie. She'd been going to school here for three months already, but had yet to make many friends. And that hurt.

Like everyone at Grimm Academy, she was a character from literature. However, while most GA students were connected with a series of tales written by the academy's founders, named Wilhelm and Jacob Grimm, her tale had been popularized by an English author named Robert Southey.

That difference had nothing to do with the reason she didn't have many friends, though. No, there were other characters here whose stories weren't written by the Grimm brothers. And there were nursery rhyme characters, too. The brothers Grimm had brought all of them to the magical realm of Grimmlandia to keep them safe from dastardly forces that could harm them. Sad to say, that safety was now being threatened — from outside Grimmlandia *and* within.

Goldie looked around the dark hall, suddenly a little creeped out by her own thoughts. She had taken a risk by coming down here tonight. But she wasn't sorry. If she succeeded in her mission, maybe other students would take notice and realize that she was a person worth befriending. A hero, in fact!

"Hey, any day now," said the goose head, interrupting

her thoughts. "Pay attention, will you? I asked you a riddle!"

"Oh, sorry," said Goldie, focusing her attention on the knob again. "Could you repeat it, please?" Students always had to correctly answer a riddle before they were allowed into the library.

The gooseknob clacked its beak in annoyance, which made the fluffy ball at the end of its polka-dot nightcap bounce up and down. "All right, but listen this time," it huffed. Then it repeated the riddle. "What has eighty-eight keys, yet cannot unlock a door?"

Goldie twisted one of her curly golden locks around a finger while she considered the riddle. "Hmm. Let's see. My aunt — the one who raised me, I mean — has this truly massive ring of keys that her housekeeper always carries around. There are keys on it for the drawing room, the kitchen, the pantry, the fourteen bedrooms, the eight bathrooms, the schoolroom where I was homeschooled, the library, and lots of other rooms, including the gardener's shed and the pool house outside."

She frowned. "But although my aunt's estate is the biggest one back in our village, I don't think even her key ring has eighty-eight keys. That's a lot!" Her blue eyes sparkled as she added, "And I'm pretty sure not a single one of her keys could *unlock* the answer to your riddle!"

It seemed that the doorknob had no sense of humor whatsoever, for it just yawned at her little joke. Then it said in a bored voice, "Hurry it up, will you? I'd like to get back to snoozing sometime in the next century."

Just then, Goldie heard the door at the end of the hall open. She darted a nervous glance in that direction, but it was too dark to see anything. "I don't have time for this," she whispered as sudden urgency filled her. "Can't you just let me in?"

Honk! "Wrong answer!" said the gooseknob, its feathers definitely ruffled by now.

"Shh!" she scolded. "Someone might hear you!"

Growing frantic, she pulled a long silver hairpin from her golden locks. At its head, white and pink pearls formed the shape of a cute flower. Holding the flower end, she poked the sharp end of the pin into the keyhole just below the gooseknob's beak. Then she moved the pin around inside the hole, feeling for the exact, precisely right spot to press so the lock would spring open.

Realizing what she was up to, the goose head cried out in a panicky voice. "Wait just a honking minute! No one gets into the library without answering a riddle." By now, it was going cross-eyed trying to see her fingers fiddling with its lock. *Honk! Honk! Honk!* "Intruder alert! Intruder alert!"

Click! At last! The lock was sprung. Instantly, the gooseknob morphed back into a silent, plain brass knob. *Ha!* She'd never yet met a lock she couldn't defeat. In fact, sometimes she just picked them for fun!

Footsteps sounded at the far end of the hallway. It was too dim to see who was coming. Which meant they couldn't see her, either. But they were getting closer.

"Hurry, hurry," she hissed under her breath, bouncing a little with impatience. It seemed to take forever, but it was probably only a few seconds later when a huge rectangle, taller and wider than she was, drew itself on the wall around the knob. A door.

She didn't take time to admire the low-relief carvings of nursery rhyme characters that decorated it, such as Little Bo Peep and her sheep and Little Boy Blue under his haystack. Instead, she yanked her hairpin out of the lock and shoved it back in her hair. Breathlessly, and taking care to not make a sound, she slipped through the door and into the library. Safe!

Once inside, Goldie looked around. The library had no windows, but a few of the chandeliers were lit with candles. Good thing, or it would've been totally dark. *Still, it's kind of eerie here at night*, she thought with a shiver. Wavery shadows loomed, cast by rows and rows of shelves housing books and all kinds of artifacts. She moved toward them.

She was breaking many rules by being here. *New* rules, mostly. Ms. Wicked's rules. Principal Rumpelstiltskin, whom most students called Principal R since using his real name caused him to throw a doozy of a temper tantrum, had mysteriously disappeared recently. He had therefore been relieved of his duties.

And for some wacky reason, the School Board had decided it would be a fine idea to put Ms. Wicked in charge of the Academy. She was also Goldie's fourth-period Scrying teacher and a real stickler for rules and security. First thing she had done was institute a curfew and install locks outside all the dorms on the fifth and sixth floors to lock students in every night at ten o'clock sharp.

Ms. Wicked had claimed it was for their own safety and that she wanted only to *protect* them. But Goldie wasn't convinced. Though she couldn't say exactly why, she didn't quite trust Ms. Wicked. Maybe it had something to do with her name. It pretty much fit her perfectly!

Bam! Her heart practically jumped out of her chest just then when the library door banged open so hard it must've hit the wall. Footsteps — more than one pair by the sounds of things — stomped inside. She got a fleeting look at figures in uniforms before she dove behind the tall checkout desk just past the entryway. *Security guards?* It was rumored that Ms. Wicked had hired some, but no one had seen them yet.

As the footsteps came toward the checkout desk, Goldie shucked off her fuzzy slippers. They had hard soles that might clack against the floor when she ran. Clutching the slippers to her chest and crouching low, she raced sound- lessly down a random aisle in her stocking feet. A short distance away she pressed her back against a shelf.

"I don't see anything amiss," she heard a deep voice say as she tried to quiet her panting breath. "Let's report back to the captain for new orders." The footsteps receded and then the library door closed and quiet fell.

Captain? They'd been security guards for sure. Not very effective ones, though. They hadn't noticed her escape. And just look how easily they'd given up searching for her!

After stepping back into her slippers, she clacked her way down the aisles of shelving. She was heading for the *G* section, which also happened to be her *G* for *goal* tonight.

Another magical thing about the Grimmstone Library was that it could vary in size from enormous to tiny, depending on its mood. Or maybe on the mood of the librarian, Ms. Goose? Tonight it was not too large and not too small, but just right, in Goldie's opinion. Which meant that it was about the size of three or four classrooms put together.

As she passed through Section *B*, she saw shelves filled with *B* things like bowling pins, bats, bells, boxes of balls . . . and a banjo! She couldn't resist picking up the banjo and strumming her fingers across its strings.

Her aunt had disapproved of most types of "entertainments and amusements" (as she called them), which basically meant anything fun. So until Goldie had come to GA she'd never played any board games or cards, and had been forbidden to dance, play, or even *listen* to music. Inside her aunt's huge mansion, there certainly hadn't been any banjos, guitars, pianos, or . . .

"*Piano!*" she exclaimed aloud. "That's the answer to the gooseknob's riddle!" She'd never been close enough to count them, but what else besides a piano would have eighty-eight keys that didn't unlock doors? Carefully, she set the banjo back on its shelf and moved on.

"Too bad you weren't able to come up with that answer before," she scolded herself. Then she gave a light laugh. "That's just like me, though. Always coming up with what I *should* have said after it's too late."

It was pretty normal for her to have conversations with herself, so she thought nothing of doing this as she scurried along. After all, she'd been left alone a lot at her aunt's and had taken to talking to herself out loud just to hear someone's voice.

She fell silent as she reached Section *G*. Here, most of the books of Grimm fairy tales were shelved. Along with other *G* items, such as various games, toy giraffes and goats, gag gifts, gadgets, gizmos, gloves, and gardening supplies.

She began to browse through the fairy-tale books. "Now, where is that Rumpelstilt . . . I mean the tale about Principal R," she said aloud as she searched for the story in book after book. Earlier that evening, she'd overheard a conversation between Malorette and Odette, two sisters who shared the dorm room right next to hers in Ruby Tower. They'd been talking and laughing about *changes* to the Rumpelstiltskin fairy tale that had "sealed the principal's fate."

Goldie figured that if she could study the tale closely, it might give her a clue about where to find him. Unlike Malorette and Odette, most everyone at GA preferred Principal R to Ms. Wicked and really wanted him back as head of the school. Including her!

She picked up a little stuffed toy giraffe and told it, "And if I can find him and bring him back . . . well . . . it might just be the *key* to becoming popular! Don't you think?" She wiggled the toy's head back and forth so it appeared to be nodding in agreement, then she set it back on its shelf.

Unfortunately, though she continued searching through every single book on the shelf, the Rumpelstiltskin tale was nowhere to be found. Not in the *G* section, anyway. "Could it have been moved to another place in the library? Or did someone check it out?" she wondered aloud.

Maybe she should just come back to the library tomorrow afternoon and ask Ms. Goose. Only she didn't really want the librarian or anyone to know what she was up to for fear someone else would get the same idea to look for Principal R and beat her to the punch. *She* wanted to be the one to find him!

She smiled to herself, imagining how students would react when she brought him back to the Academy. "Oh, Goldie," they'd say. "You're our hero! We're so grateful to you for finding him!" And, "We've never met anyone as clever as you are!" Then they'd beg her to go do stuff with them and she'd get a flood of invitations to picnics and parties and the like. "I'll have to check my schedule first to see if I can fit that in," she'd say.

Bam! Just then, the door to the library slammed open again. More footsteps. Instinctively, Goldie dropped to a crouch. "G*rrr*eat gobs of gopher guts!" a deep, voice growled. "I *smell* somebody."

Oh, no! More guards! she thought. But — *smelled somebody?* Did she need to take a shower?

Then another voice, this one kind of high-pitched and squeaky, asked, "Is it us?"

"Don't be ridiculous," said a medium-pitched, lady-like voice. "Of course it's not us! Bears always smell good. It's just the smell of GA students. It's all over the Academy."

Bears? thought Goldie. What were these guards talking about?

"I'll do a sweep of Sections *A* to *I*. You take *J* to *Q*," the deep-voiced guard said gruffly to one of the others. Goldie didn't know which one because she couldn't see them. And she didn't think she'd better risk peeking out to *try*.

"Guess that leaves me with *R* to *Z*," grumbled the squeaky-voiced guard, who sounded younger than the other two.

"G*rrr*eat!" the deep voice of the growly guard said with enthusiasm. "Let's go!"

Goldie looked around the *G* section wildly. Where oh where could she hide? She didn't know what the penalty for breaking curfew was, but Ms. Wicked had implied during her daily announcements this morning that it would be something really awful. Scrubbing the dungeon floors, perhaps? Cleaning out the huge hot baking ovens in the kitchen for Mistress Hagscorch, the Academy's scary Head Cook?

Or maybe Ms. Wicked would make sure that students who were caught out after curfew would simply mysteriously disappear, just as Principal R had! Goldie's heart beat faster as footsteps came closer. Her plan to come here had been full of holes. And she had a hole in her head to even *think* it could have succeeded.

2

Holing Up

*H*oles? *That's it!* thought Goldie. Before any of the guards could catch sight of her, she ran ahead to the *H* section.

There, as she'd hoped, she found holes of all shapes and sizes. Maybe one of them would be big enough to hide in. The doughnut holes were too small, though she did eat several. After all, who was going to notice a few missing? The holes in the hunk of Swiss cheese were even smaller than the doughnut holes. So were the buttonholes and pigeonholes. The cubbyholes were bigger, but not big enough. She was getting desperate.

As footsteps came closer, she suddenly spied a hole in the wall about two feet off the ground and to her left. The label below the hole read A HOLE LOT OF NOTHING. Well, maybe she could fill it with something. Herself!

Grabbing on to the top edge of the hole's opening, she swung herself through, feet first. For once, she was glad to be small. The hole proved to be just big enough for her to wiggle through. She scooched down inside the void behind it in the nick of time, managing to twist herself into a comfortable crouch.

Was it dark enough inside her hidey-hole so that she wouldn't be detected? She held her breath as she waited to see what would happen.

She didn't have to wait long. Footsteps turned and came closer, and closer. All of a sudden, she spied fuzzy feet standing in the aisle right next to her. They were attached to fuzzy legs. *Huh?* She scooched forward a bit and lifted her head to see more. A *bear?* An actual bear as tall as a grown-up? *Yikes!* When one of the guards had said that bears always smell good, it was a reference to themselves!

And that explained why the guards had sounded so growly. Luckily, this bear was looking at something on a shelf across from where she was hiding, not at her. He was dressed in a dark blue guard uniform with short pants and a jacket. And when he turned sideways, she saw that the jacket had big brass buttons down the front of it. Quickly and quietly, she scooted backward, curling deeper into her hidey-hole.

"Hic. Hic." *Holey* hiccups! She'd come down with them at the exact wrong moment. That's what she got for eating those doughnut holes in the middle of the night. Goldie clapped both hands over her mouth, but it was too late. The guard had heard her.

He wheeled around. "Who's the*rrr*e?" he growled in his loud, deep voice. When he glanced right at the hole in the wall, she thought she was in for it for sure. *Oh, no!* He was going to discover her, tell Ms. Wicked, and she'd probably find herself chained up in the school dungeon for rule breaking. Or worse!

As more footsteps came running, the guard began to chuckle. *Harrr! Harrr!* He slapped his fuzzy knee as if he'd just heard the best joke ever.

Two more bears appeared — a small one about her height and a medium-size one. They were in uniform as well. And, except for their different sizes, all three were identical. *Hmm.* There was something kind of familiar-looking about all of them.

"What's so funny?" asked the other two guards.

The biggest guard's laughter died away. "I hea*rrr*d hiccups," he said, "but then I realized I was in the *H* aisle. And there's a box labeled HICCUPS *rrr*ight up there." He pointed a shaggy paw toward the shelf just above Goldie's hidey-hole.

Phew, she thought in relief. Saved from discovery by a box of hiccups! Right when she had gotten a case of them herself.

"Oh, Teddy, you're such a goofball," said the medium-size bear.

"*Shhh!* No real names," growled the big bear. "While we're at the Academy, we only use the code names Principal W assigned us, remember? I'm Papa Bear. And you're Mama Bear. And you're Baby Bear. Got it?"

"Got it!" said the other two guards, straightening and saluting.

So Ms. Wicked was calling herself Principal W now, was she? mused Goldie. Even though the School Board had only named her the *acting* principal, and she was actually still a teacher?

Just then the big Papa Bear guard's stomach growled. "I'm hungry as, well, as a bear. We've checked all the sections. Let's go get the boat and head home," he told the others. "Principal W told us a special visitor will be waiting for us the*rrr*e, remember?"

Special visitor? At this, Goldie's ears perked up. Who could it be? Ms. Wicked herself? Another guard? Since the bears were taking a boat to get home, did that mean they were living on one of the islands in the Once Upon River? Maze Island? Heart Island? So many questions. And to her, they were like locks. She always wanted to pick them open to find answers!

Moments later, she heard the library's door open and shut. When all seemed quiet, she inched her way out of the hole, unable to *bear* another moment in hiding. Though disappointed that she hadn't been able to find any clues to Principal R's whereabouts, at least she now knew something about Ms. Wicked's guards.

And most importantly she hadn't been discovered. Which was weird because that Papa Bear guard had been looking right at her when she was inside the hidey-hole. Why hadn't he seen her, or at least smelled her? She'd heard that bears' noses were better at sniffing out smells than people's noses were. Even better than a bloodhound's.

As her feet found the floor and she stood again, her gaze fell once more on the label below the hole. "A hole lot of nothing," she murmured to herself. *Maybe that was the answer!* No matter what got stashed inside this hole — including her — all that anyone outside it could sense was . . . well . . . *nothing.*

Which was exactly what Goldie hoped to see as she wound her way out of the library, then raced upstairs. Nothing and no one. And it seemed luck was with her for she saw no guards, no teachers, and no students all the way up to the dorms.

On the sixth floor, she had to cross an outdoor stone walkway that ran between all three of the Pink Castle's towers to get back to her room. Outside, the night air was cool and the moon shone brightly in the sky above the pointy-top towers. One of them was a pale, frosty white —

Pearl Tower. Another was a sparkly green — Emerald Tower. And the third was a dazzling red. That was Ruby Tower. Her dorm. Across the river at Gray Castle, the pointy tops of the boys' dorm towers gleamed with jewel colors, too — Onyx, Topaz, and Zircon.

She paused to peek over the side of the walkway. Below her, in a courtyard between the rest of the girls' dorms on the fifth floor, she could just make out a tall, three-tiered fountain where a mermaid girl named Mermily always slept. Far, far below that, the moon's reflection wavered on the waters of the Once Upon River. It was a beautiful and reassuringly peaceful sight, untouched by the troubling changes Ms. Wicked had begun to make at the Academy ever since she was appointed acting principal.

When Goldie finally arrived at the door to Ruby Tower, she was relieved to see the key was still there, just as she'd left it. Though it was now school policy for students to be locked in their dorms at night, the key always remained stuck in the outside lock.

To get out of the dorm that night, she had simply used her pearl-flower hairpin on the inside lock to push this key out. She'd caught it on a flat sheet of vellum she had shoved under the door and out onto the walkway, then slid the vellum back inside with the key lying upon it. Once outside, she'd put the key back in the lock so all would look undisturbed.

As she reached for the key to unlock the tower door, she heard a commotion behind her. "Get back to your post!" someone shouted. She froze. Had she been spotted by a guard? Trembling, she glanced over her shoulder, but saw no one.

A second voice called out, "Papa Bear assigned me to this spot. You're the one in the wrong place. You're supposed to be patrolling the *sixth* floor."

Phew. The voices were coming from the fifth-floor courtyard, not right behind her as she'd first supposed. And it sounded like Papa Bear must be the Head Guard, in charge of the other two bear guards down there and any others Ms. Wicked might have hired.

Curious to know if these other guards were also bears, she risked a quick peek over the side of the walkway. The fifth-floor guard's back was to her. But she could see at a glance that he wasn't a bear. There was a fluffy orange tail with a white tip sticking out of the back of his uniform. A fox!

Hearing footsteps on the stairs, she darted back to the tower door and fumbled with the key. For one heart-stopping moment, she couldn't get it to turn in the lock. When it finally did, she leaped over the doorstep, and then shut the door softly behind her. *Snick!*

All was quiet inside the circular dorm, which was ringed with little sleeping alcoves. The one Goldie shared with her roommate, Polly, was just to the left of the door, so she didn't even need to walk through the common area at the center of the dorm to get to it. She pushed aside the decorative ruby-studded curtain at the entrance to her shared little bedroom. Then she shucked off her slippers, picked them up, and tiptoed inside.

The moon shone through the window on the far wall, casting light on the multicolored braided rug that lay between the two canopy beds with pretty see-through fabric draped across their tops. Both beds were raised about six feet off the floor on tall bedposts to accommodate desks beneath them. As she bent to set her slippers next to her desk, one of them fell from her arms and thumped onto the floor.

"Goldie?" Polly called out sleepily. "Is it morning already? Want me to make us a pot of tea?"

The corners of Goldie's mouth lifted into a grin. Her roomie was obsessed with tea. She couldn't help it, though. She was one of the nursery rhyme characters brought here to Grimmlandia for protection long ago, and the first verse of her rhyme went like this:

> *Polly, put the kettle on,*
> *Polly, put the kettle on,*
> *Polly, put the kettle on,*
> *And let's drink tea.*

"Shh," she told Polly. "It's not morning yet. Go back to sleep."

Polly mumbled something that sounded like "Darjeeling or Earl Grey?" which Goldie knew by now were two popular kinds of tea. And then the girl rolled over and began to softly snore.

Goldie bent to straighten her slippers. As she stood, her eyes chanced to fall on a pair of matching two-inch tall teddy bears nestled on either side of the candlestick on her desktop. Hey! Despite their teeny size, those teddy bears looked exactly like the bears in the library. Same cute ears. Same shiny brown fur. Same round, brown eyes. Only, her bears weren't wearing uniforms. They also weren't *alive*.

She picked them up to look at them more closely. Weeks ago, both had sprouted from a magical tongue-twister plant she'd grown in Ms. Blue Fairygodmother's Bespellings class. Each student in class had created one of the special plants as a decoration for a student-run festival out on Heart Island. A festival meant to raise funds for the always cash-strapped Academy. Goldie had been hopeful her plant might be judged the best at the festival and win a prize, but no such luck.

She turned the small toy bears over in the palm of her hand. They were really quite cute if she did say so herself. After the festival ended, she'd retrieved her plant, intending to pick off and keep the stuffed bear blossoms and the fuzzy toy fox blossoms she'd grown. However, all had disappeared. Except these two. They'd been tucked under some leaves near the base of the plant and must've been overlooked by whoever had snitched the rest.

Other students' plants had been stripped of blossoms, too. They figured it must've been village children who'd plucked the cute blossoms from all the plants. But . . . *wait a minute! Bears and foxes!* Like those guards!

Her mind raced, connecting the dots. Could Ms. Wicked have taken the magical blossoms? Back when Principal R was still around, had she cast a magic spell to make the blossoms larger and more alive, turning them into her own personal army of school security guards? Why would a teacher make plans to raise an army of guards before knowing the principal was going to disappear though? Unless . . . had she maybe been the very person who'd plotted the principal's downfall? The thought was so alarming that it made Goldie gasp.

Bong! Bong! Bong! The grandfather clock over in the Great Hall sounded the hour with twelve bongs. Midnight.

"Orange spice? Chai? Black pekoe?" Polly murmured in her sleep. More tea flavors.

"Shhh," Goldie soothed, and her roomie went back to snoozing. She set the tiny toy bears back on her desk and moved to the ladder at the end of her bed. She'd left her room at midnight and had been in the library for a while, of course. However, another odd thing about the Grimmstone Library was that time could move much slower or faster inside it than in the rest of the Academy and Grimmlandia.

Lucky for her, time had moved slowly inside the library tonight so that only a few minutes had gone by in the outside world. Which meant she was going to get a proper amount of sleep.

After climbing up the ladder to her tall canopy bed, she snuggled under her blue-and-green-checkered comforter and was soon fast asleep.

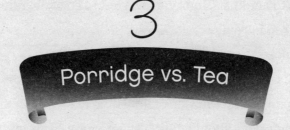

3

Porridge vs. Tea

At breakfast the next morning, Goldie took a seat on a bench next to Polly, and across from Malorette and Odette at one of the two long dining tables that ran the length of the Great Hall. Two stories high, this Hall straddled the Once Upon River and connected the two castles at either end of the Academy. Colorful banners graced its walls, and bluebirds constantly flittered in and out of its high, open windows, which had beautiful diamond-shaped glass panes.

"Ow! This stuff is too hot," Goldie complained when she took a spoonful of her oatsqueal porridge.

Polly's long blond hair, done up in a perky ponytail, swished from side to side as she shook her head, eyeing Goldie's bowl. "Don't you ever get tired of eating porridge?" she teased in a friendly way as Goldie mixed a spoonful of brown sugar into the steaming hot oatsqueal. As usual, it made a shrill sound like a cross between a badly played violin and a whistle as she stirred the sugar into it.

Goldie glanced over at the cup of tea Polly had just raised to her lips. "Don't you ever get tired of drinking tea?" she asked in reply.

Malorette and Odette both cackled. "She's got you there," Odette said to Polly, who blushed as pink as the roses painted on the side of her china teacup.

"Yeah, you should talk," Malorette added, giving her poofy black hair a pat. "You and your endless pots of tea."

Seemingly recovered from her initial embarrassment, Polly shrugged. "Tea is a very versatile beverage," she said. "And there are endless varieties. Besides all the kinds of black teas, there are also herbal teas like chamomile, peppermint, orange blossom, and blueberry. I could go on and on about —"

"Oh! Please don't!" Malorette said, arching an eyebrow in a sarcastic way.

Odette cackled again.

"Huh? I was just —" Polly stopped, glancing over at Goldie for support.

But Goldie had no idea what Polly wanted her to say. "What?" she said, wrinkling her forehead in confusion.

"Nothing," Polly said with a sigh.

Goldie had a feeling she'd somehow let her roomie down. However, Malorette smiled at her as if suddenly greatly pleased with her for some reason. "Odette and I are going to take a boat over to Maze Island after school this afternoon. Want to come with?"

"Me? With you guys? Sure," Goldie said in eager surprise. No one at GA ever asked her to do anything with them. Well, sometimes Polly did, but she kind of had to because she'd gotten stuck with her as a roommate.

Goldie stared at the two sisters, hoping this wasn't some kind of trick where they wouldn't show up, and then laugh at her for thinking they had ever meant to. But she'd take the chance. Besides, she'd already been thinking she should go over to that island to snoop around for security guard cottages.

"Wait. Isn't going there against Ms. Wicked's new rules? She said no one could leave the school grounds," Polly said, sounding a little anxious. *Or maybe a little jealous?* wondered Goldie.

"Neverwood Forest and the rest of Grimmlandia are out of bounds," said Odette. "But Maze Island, Heart Island, and the Once Upon River are all part of the Academy."

"Oh," said Polly. She flushed again, as if she'd just suffered an embarrassing put-down.

Fearful that she'd been unintentionally rude to Polly (what else was new?), Goldie tried to catch her roommate's eye so she could smile an apology. But Polly was fixedly staring into her teacup. Even when Goldie nudged her elbow, her roomie wouldn't look up. Then Mermily, who was sitting on Polly's other side, started to talk to her, and the moment for apologizing was lost.

"So we'll meet you down by the boats after sixth period?" Odette was asking now.

Goldie nodded distractedly. "Sure. I don't have anything better to do." That was true, but possibly not the best, most flattering reply she could've made.

Malorette and Odette both did a double take. *Great. Just great. I've done it again,* she thought. What was wrong with her? Her mouth was like a volcano sometimes, erupting without warning. Her tongue flapped like a flag on a flagpole. *See?* She was even rude to herself sometimes. *Argh!*

Ruefully, she recalled the gooseknob commenting that her bad habit of nearly always saying what she thought probably didn't win her a lot of friends. Aside from Polly, who kind of had to be her friend since they were room-mates, Malorette and Odette were the only other girls at GA who were halfway interested in hanging out with her.

Yes, they were evil characters in literature, and maybe that didn't say much for Goldie's social skills. Still, fairy tales were made up of good and bad. You couldn't exclude half of the characters from school or nobody's story would make sense.

She didn't want to blow her chances at a new friendship, even one with evil characters. Worried the two sisters might take back their invitation, Goldie belatedly added, "I'm really jazzed about going to the island with you guys. Thanks. It'll be fun!" It must've been the right thing to say because Odette and Malorette were suddenly all smiles again.

Just then, trumpets blared. *Ta*-ta-ta-*ta*-ta-ta-*tum!* Two musicians had appeared on the second-floor balcony that overlooked the east end of the Great Hall. As soon as they lowered their long, thin, golden herald trumpets, the five shiny iron helmet-heads that sat on a wide, carved wooden shelf on the stone wall behind them began to speak.

"Attention, scholars!" they chorused in formal-sounding voices. Their visors creaked and clanked open and shut as they spoke, and the colored feather that stuck up from the top of each one's helmet bobbed up and down. "All rise for today's announcements from the great and goodly principal of Grimm Academy!" they called out.

Goldie stood, along with all the other students. The disembodied helmet-heads' appearance was a bit startling, even in a place as magical as Grimmlandia. However, she'd now had three whole months to get used to the fact that they were, in fact, the GA School Board. And it was they who had made the decision to relieve Principal R of his duties after his disappearance and put Ms. Wicked in charge — for the time being.

Click! Click! Click! The sound of high heels echoed throughout the Hall as Ms. Wicked stepped onto the balcony. Slender and tall, she had perfectly styled black hair piled high inside a tiara with points so sharp they looked like dragons' teeth.

This Scrying-teacher-turned-principal had no need of the small stepladder Principal R had always climbed to make himself visible above the balcony railing when he spoke to the students each morning. But then, he had been, er, was (she wasn't really sure which was right since no one knew if he'd ever return), a gnome. No more than three feet tall, including his tall hat.

"Good morning, students!" Ms. Wicked said in a clear, crisp voice. She smiled wide as her eyes swept the Hall.

Goldie shivered. There was something not quite right about the way that woman smiled. Though her smiles were wide and white, they never reached her eyes and weren't at all warm. In fact, they were downright cold. Instead of nice — they were *ice*. Which is probably why they made her shiver.

"In Principal R's absence, all volunteer efforts to try to spin a certain magical straw into gold will henceforth be abandoned," Ms. Wicked went on. "So anyone who has signed up to try their hand at spinning need not report to Ms. Queenharts or myself." She was referring to the legendary Straw of Gold that Principal R had hoped would end the Academy's financial problems once and for all.

"When will Principal R be back?" a girl in a red cloak with red-streaked dark hair dared to call out. Her name was Red Riding Hood. Goldie didn't know her all that well, even though they were in Ms. Wicked's fourth-period Scrying class together. But pretty much everyone found Red interesting. She was popular and talented, in a dramatic sort of way. Which was the reason she'd landed the starring role in the drama class's recent production of a play called *Red Robin Hood*.

In Goldie's opinion, she had played the part not too woodenly, not too flamboyantly . . . but just right. A new play by some guy named Shakespeare was being cast now, and Red would probably land a starring role in that, too.

A scowl had flickered across Ms. Wicked's face at Red's question. But now she smiled again. "Naturally, we all hope he'll return soon," she said in a syrupy-sweet voice. "But as to when that might be, well, we'll just have to wait and see. And that will be one demerit for the callout, young lady." At this, Red's BFFs, Cinderella, Rapunzel, and Snow White, sent her sympathetic looks.

Reaching up to pat her already perfect hair, Ms. Wicked changed the subject. "Now, I've heard some grumbling about the heightened security measures. As I've said before, such measures are absolutely necessary for the protection of everyone here." *Bam!* She pounded a fist on the railing, causing everyone, including the musicians with their trumpets, to jump. "There's reason to believe that just last night an unknown intruder entered the library after curfew," she announced.

This elicited nervous and even frightened murmurs and rustling from the students. From behind Goldie, Polly whispered, "Wow, I guess we really do need protection." Goldie had a feeling that making everyone nervous was exactly Ms. Wicked's aim. If she could keep them fearful, she might be able to distract them from asking any more questions about Principal R or arguing with her rules.

When Ms. Wicked's cold, accusing gaze swept over the students, Goldie's eyes went wide. She scooched over a tad to hide behind Rapunzel, the girl standing ahead of her. Had the gooseknob told on her? If so, it couldn't have revealed her name. She was pretty sure it didn't know it.

Now that she'd pretty much made this into a not-grimmtastic morning for everyone, Ms. Wicked was suddenly all smiles again. "Never fear, students. To help enforce the new rules — especially the nightly curfew and the need to stay within the Academy's boundaries — I've engaged a talented team of guards to keep us all safe." Glancing down to the open doors at the opposite end of the Great Hall, she called out, "Guards! Enter, please!"

Apparently, a whole team of guards had been quietly waiting outside the far end of the Hall for her cue, because now they burst in through the tall doors. Led by Papa Bear, with Mama Bear and Baby Bear directly behind him, the guards moved in perfect formation. Five lines of four guards each, they trooped right down the center of the Hall between the two long tables of students. *Hop! Clomp! Scamper! Stomp!*

All the guards were animals, and wore navy blue uniforms of short pants and jackets with shiny brass buttons. Goldie did her times tables and quickly figured there were twenty of them. Plus the three bear leaders. Which was a lot of guards for one school.

She counted two kangaroos, three jackrabbits, four foxes (the same number that had been on her tongue-twister plant!), four zebras, three beavers, two anteaters, and two badgers. Once they'd marched, hopped, and scampered the full length of the Hall, the guards finally came to a halt at the east end. There, they formally saluted Ms. Wicked.

"Marvelous, aren't they?" she crowed. Again, her eyes

swept the entire room. "Make no mistake, students. For your own good, and the safety of everyone here at GA, anyone caught breaking the rules from now on will face dire consequences. Including time in the dungeon to contemplate their mistakes, and probable expulsion from the Academy." She paused to let that sink in. Then she added, "And if anyone sees anyone else breaking the rules, or has information that might lead to the capture of last night's intruder, it is your duty to come forward. Be assured that informers will be amply rewarded."

Goldie gulped. Could she really be one hundred percent certain that none of the girls in her Ruby Tower dorm — or anyone else in the Academy — had seen her leaving or returning after curfew last night? *No*, she thought, clasping her hands together in the folds of her gown to hide the fact that they were shaking. She really couldn't.

"Oh, and have a happily-ever-after day," Ms. Wicked cooed to them all at last.

Huh? Was she kidding? Not a chance after that speech, thought Goldie.

4

Bubbles!

After that rocky start to the day, students were pretty glum and on edge all morning. Goldie kept her eyes peeled for the library gooseknob, especially on the way to her third-period Bespellings and Enchantments class. However, the knob was no longer where it had been the night before. So the library had already moved elsewhere.

Good, she thought. She'd been a little afraid that if she passed the knob, it might morph into a goose head again, remember her, and rat her out as the intruder in the library after curfew last night!

In Bespellings and Enchantments, three long tables were lined up one behind another as usual, facing the teacher's desk at the front of the room. Goldie's table was at the back. As she passed the middle table, several boys (most of them princes) were laughing and talking loudly. One of them, the unfortunately named Prince Foulsmell, glanced up. He wore a simple gold crown atop his tousled brown hair. Just in case he was going to smile at her, she quickly looked away before he could.

On her first day at GA, Malorette had warned her never, ever to smile at this prince. "If you do, he'll follow you around like a puppy forever after," she'd said. Well, that was something Goldie definitely didn't need or want! So she never had smiled at him. However, she had sniffed in his direction once, and discovered for herself that he smelled neither foul nor sweet, but pretty much just right for a boy.

As she took her seat in the back, the teacher floated up to the front of the room inside a huge bubble of pale blue light. "A magical good morning to you all, class!" Ms. Blue Fairygodmother trilled. The bubble extended with her hand as she tapped her wand on her desk to get everyone's attention. Then she said, "Open your Handbooks to Chapter Eleven, please."

The chapter was titled "Defensive Magic," Goldie discovered. It appeared to be about ways to protect yourself from the effects of harmful spells. Strangely enough, its first section was called "Bubble-making." *Huh?*

"Today we'll be learning about protective bubbles," Ms. Blue Fairygodmother said before Goldie could puzzle it out for herself. "*My* bubble, for example, is much stronger than it looks. While I am floating around inside it, nothing and no one can hurt me. It's practically indestructible."

Prince Foulsmell smiled goofily and his hand shot in the air. "Can I test that?"

Goldie sucked in her breath. Her aunt would have called his question impertinent and disrespectful — accusations she'd leveled at Goldie on more than one occasion.

However, Ms. Blue was unfazed. "Sure," she said, gesturing for him to come up to the front of the classroom. "Do your worst."

With a determined look on his face, Foulsmell went up and gave the big blue bubble a poke with the sharp point of a feather pen. The pen dented the bubble for a few seconds. However, when he pulled the pen away, the bubble sprang back into its original shape, unharmed.

Switching tactics, he charged at the bubble, launching himself against it. "*Whoa!*" he called out in surprise as he bounced off its surface and away again. His arms cartwheeled crazily as he flew through the air, somehow managing to land on the floor in a crouch. Straightening, he turned toward the class, posing triumphantly. "Yes! I *nailed* that landing!"

Seeing that he was all right, everyone laughed and clapped. "That's some tough bubble," one of his friends called out to Ms. Blue in an admiring tone. She just smiled.

As Foulsmell returned to his seat, Ms. Blue handed practice wands around to everyone. "You are to practice making protective bubbles using the instructions in your Handbooks," she told the class. "But first choose a partner so you can help each other as needed."

Hearing that last part, Goldie's heart sank. In her three months at the Academy, she'd always been chosen last whenever they did pair or group activities in any of her classes. Too bad there wasn't a bubble that could protect *feelings*. Then maybe during those times, her feelings of being left out and friendless would just bounce off her!

Already, students were pairing up. Determined not to be left out this time, Goldie scrambled to ask Mermily, who sat at her table. A split second before she could, however, Mary Mary Quite Contrary popped over to claim the mermaid as *her* partner.

Goldie thought next of asking Rapunzel. Gathering her courage, she went over to the goth-looking girl whose long blue-streaked black hair grew so rapidly it sometimes touched the floor. "Want to be my partner?" she asked.

"Oh, sorry," said Rapunzel kindly. "Basil already asked."

Basil was Rapunzel's crush, and sat at the same table. If only Goldie had remembered that. Naturally, they'd partner up. What an idiot she was not to think of it before coming over! "S'okay," she mumbled.

Panicky feelings welled up inside her as she glanced around the room, looking for someone else to ask. But, things were looking *grimm*. Everywhere she looked, pairs, pairs, pairs! Argh! It would be awful if she wound up having to work with Ms. Blue. Nothing quite said "loser" like having to partner with a teacher because no one else picked you.

Not that she didn't like Ms. Blue. She was actually her favorite teacher. When Goldie had first arrived at GA (without any fanfare or hoopla since she wasn't royalty), she'd come with a trunkful of dull gray dresses her aunt had considered "practical and appropriate." In other words, ugly!

Ms. Blue was the only teacher who had seemed to take notice of her drab attire. She'd spotted Goldie in the library one day, trying (and failing) to use a magic mirror there to make herself new gowns. "Oh!" the teacher had said. "I was just coming to use the mirror to work on my gown-making skills. Why don't you let me make some gowns for you? It would be such fun!" Then the teacher had proceeded to conjure up a whole new wardrobe of beautiful everyday gowns to replace Goldie's gray ones.

Ms. Blue had even made her a couple of ball gowns. Goldie didn't have the heart to tell her that she wasn't planning on going to any balls. She had been to one the night after she enrolled at GA. No one had asked her to dance and she'd been too chicken to ask anyone, either. It had been both grimmorrible and grimmbarrassing! Not an experience she ever planned to repeat. She remembered waiting and hoping for some boy to come along and . . .

Just then a tap came on her shoulder. She whirled around to see that Prince Foulsmell had tapped her with his wand. "What did you do that for?" she demanded, sensing a possible joke at her expense.

"Presto! Chango!" he replied goofily, tapping her again. "You are now turned into my partner. C'mon." With that, he spun around and went back to his desk, obviously expecting her to follow. She hesitated, torn. He was more popular than she was (who wasn't?). But his goofy humor was something she wasn't at all used to and didn't know how to deal with, having been raised by her strict, no-nonsense aunt.

On the other hand, partnering with him was her best option right now if she didn't want to have to partner with a teacher. Which she didn't. Deciding to take a chance on the puppy-dog thing, she trailed after him. It wasn't like she had any better offers to consider!

"Okay," Foulsmell began once they stood together at his desk. "My Handbook says that creating perfect bubbles is a snap."

"Yeah, uh-huh," Goldie said skeptically. As she expected, it wasn't as easy as their Handbook instructions made it sound. The first bubble she made covered only her bottom half, and it swung her around so she was floating upside down with her feet in the air. She was more than a little annoyed when Foulsmell laughed as she struggled to keep her skirt in place.

"You're not exactly an expert at this, either, grape boy!" she said crossly as they each grabbed the edge of his desk to right themselves. His bottom half was encased in a purple-colored bubble he'd made that had also upended him. Once they were both right side up again, she poked her magic wand at her bubble. *Pop!* Turned out that protective bubbles could be popped only by the person who created them.

"Isn't getting good at it the whole *point* of this exercise?" Foulsmell replied good-naturedly. As he said the word *point*, he stuck the point of his wand into his own bubble, popping it. *Eew!* For some reason, his bubble exploded, coating him with a sticky purple goo that made him resemble something halfway between a gigantic plum and a monstrous raisin.

Instead of getting mad, he just licked a drip of goo off his fingertip. "Mmm. Grape," he said.

Goldie couldn't help laughing at his remark. In fact, many of the other students in class were laughing with equal parts delight and frustration as their bubbles stuck to the ceiling, bounced them around the room, unexpectedly exploded, or took on weird shapes.

"You're doing great, everyone," Ms. Blue called out as she floated here and there to offer tips. Including how to magically remove the goo after an accidental bubble explosion. "If your first efforts seem like flops, don't worry," she told them. "Like most things, bubble magic requires lots of practice."

Encouraged, Goldie tried again. Her second bubble did turn out a little better. Though it was bright red and rather flat on the bottom and lumpy on top, at least it covered all of her.

Foulsmell regarded her critically. "You look kind of like one of Mistress Hagscorch's Heart-of-Despairberry Tarts," he teased.

"Thanks a lot," grumped Goldie. Apparently, she wasn't the only one with a bad habit of blurting out exactly what she thought.

A friend of his, Prince Awesome, bounced over in his bubble just then and overheard. "That's a compliment, coming from him. He *loves* those tarts!" the prince informed Goldie.

"Ha-ha! What a bunch of bubbleoney," said Foulsmell, giving him and his bubble a push off. However, as Prince Awesome bounced back to his partner, a blush crept from

Foulsmell's neck to his cheeks and up to the roots of his tangled hair. Quickly, he created another bubble around himself, as if for protection against whatever she might say back.

Was it the word *love* that had made him blush? Goldie reached with her wand to burst her bubble. He couldn't have a crush on her, could he? Though she felt a little alarmed at the idea, she also felt flattered. To her knowledge, no boy had ever had a crush on her. Not that she'd been around many of them before coming to GA, of course. But she suspected that her tart tongue kept most boys at bay, the same way it seemed to do with potential new friends.

Before she could come up with anything to say to Foulsmell, the classroom door flew open. And there stood Ms. Wicked. Er, Principal Wicked. No! Goldie refused to think of her as the *actual* principal.

Ms. Blue was busy helping to separate two girls whose bubbles had stuck together, so she didn't notice when the new arrival clicked her way into the room. A sour expression came over Ms. Wicked's face as she stood for a couple of minutes observing the lesson.

"What's her problem?" Foulsmell wondered quietly.

"No clue," Goldie replied with a shrug.

"Ahem!" Ms. Wicked said loudly. All chatter within the classroom instantly stopped.

Ms. Blue whirled around inside her bubble. "Oh! I'm sorry," she said at once. "I didn't hear you come in."

"We need to talk," Ms. Wicked said abruptly. "Outside in the hallway, please. *Now.*"

The students all stared at one another as Ms. Blue followed Ms. Wicked out the door. Then they went back to practicing. The period was nearly at an end when Ms. Blue reentered the classroom. Normally unflappable, she now looked quite shaken.

"I wonder what Ms. Wicked said to her," Goldie whispered to Foulsmell, who was encased in a wobbly bubble that resembled a giant jellyfish.

"Good question," he replied. He popped his bubble, but then had to battle his way out of it since the top half had stuck to him.

A few minutes later the clock began to bong and class let out. Goldie hadn't quite gotten the hang of bubble-making, but she was surprised how much fun she'd had trying.

"Hey, wait up," Foulsmell called to Goldie as she left the room. Catching up to her outside the door, he fell into step beside her on the way to the Great Hall for lunch. *Uh-oh,* thought Goldie. Was this the kind of thing Malorette had tried to warn her about? Was he going to follow her around like a puppy now?

But she wanted friends, right? And Foulsmell's goofy cuteness was growing on her. He had turned out to be both funny and fun. Ignoring Malorette's warning, she found herself blurting, "Do you think Ms. Blue chose this week to teach us defensive magic so we could protect ourselves from Ms. Wicked and her guards? I mean, Ms. Wicked *is* an evil villain in the Grimm fairy tales. And it wasn't that long ago — right before Principal R's disappearance, as a matter of fact — that he told us about E.V.I.L.'s existence and warned us to be extra vigilant."

E.V.I.L., which stood for Exceptional Villains in Literature, was a secret society that had flourished during the Dark Ages but had been defunct until recently. Though Principal R hadn't made the group's aims very clear, he'd stated plainly that they were up to no good and would be happy to see the Academy fail.

"You think Ms. Wicked *wants* us all to be vulnerable to E.V.I.L.?" Foulsmell asked.

"Maybe. Just like she wants to control where we go and what we do by hiring all those animal guards and locking us in at night," said Goldie.

Foulsmell just shrugged, maddeningly unconcerned. "I prefer to give her the benefit of the doubt," he said as they neared the Hall for lunch. "Being suspicious of people isn't a very fun way to live, in my humble opinion."

"I'm going to have to change your name to *Fool*smell if that's the way you think," she said, half teasing and half serious. Immediately after the words left her mouth, she stiffened. *I did it again!* she scolded herself. *Said the first rude thing that popped into my head.*

However, Foulsmell just grinned. "Sure. If you think that's a better name for me." Though he didn't *sound* mad, what if she'd really hurt him and he was only covering up his feelings? Had she blown this chance at making a friend?

A uniformed beaver guard with large, prominent teeth was lurking just outside the entrance to the Great Hall. As Goldie and Foulsmell approached, the beaver bent to pick up a pencil that someone had dropped, and then started to munch it. Suddenly, Ms. Wicked appeared. Pointing a finger with a red sharp-tipped fingernail at him, she exclaimed, "You there! You're supposed to be monitoring for suspicious behavior, not devouring school supplies. Stop snacking and get cracking!"

Goldie and Foulsmell exchanged a grin as the hapless beaver ducked its head and muttered an apology, while at the same time tucking the remainder of the pencil into its jacket pocket. Embroidered on the pocket of his uniform was a large *W* with a thorny vine woven through it, Goldie now noticed. Was the thorny *W* a logo Ms. Wicked had created for herself? *Great Grimmlets!*

Once inside the Hall, a couple of Foulsmell's friends called out that they'd saved him a place in line. He wiggled his eyebrows at Goldie. "So long, bubble buddy," he said to her. Grinning, he turned and sprinted across the room to join the other boys.

Must be nice to have friends call you over to hang with them, she thought, watching him go. As she stood in the line, she thought over what he'd said. Was he right about giving others the benefit of the doubt and not being suspicious of everyone? With a sigh, she decided his kind of gullible thinking could get you in trouble. After all, Principal R wouldn't have given his warning about E.V.I.L. if he weren't suspicious of the group. For at least the hundredth time since his disappearance, she wondered where he could possibly be.

5

Maze Island

There was a four-foot-tall, jittery-looking jackrabbit standing guard at the end of the Pink Castle drawbridge. Goldie spotted it as she began to cross over after classes were finally out for the day. "H-h-halt! Who goes there?" it cried, jumping to block her path. Its nose twitched and its ears stood straight up as it spoke. "State your n-name and d-destination."

"My name is Goldie and I'm meeting two girls to take a boat to Maze Island," she said. "We're still allowed to visit the islands, right?" She wouldn't have put it past Ms. Wicked to tighten the rules even further without warning anyone — but only "*for everyone's safety,*" of course. *Ha!*

"Yes. You may g-go," replied the rabbit, moving aside. "As long as you're b-back before d-dark."

"No problem," said Goldie, starting to pass. Then she paused. "Hey, where do all you guards stay when you're not on duty?"

"S-secret locations in Gray C-castle," said the guard.

Goldie frowned. "The bears, too?"

Suddenly, the jackrabbit regarded her with suspicion. "Wh-why do you ask?"

Just then, some boys out on the Academy lawn shot a large rotten squash from a catapult. *Smack!* The sound of the squash hitting the side of the school startled the jittery jackrabbit so much that he jumped as high as the second-story windows.

Before he could land, Goldie dashed across the draw-bridge so he wouldn't be able to question her further. The bears in the library had said they were staying on an island. Why weren't all the guards staying together? Were the bears guarding something? The principal maybe? Excitement filled her. Maybe she'd wind up a hero this very day. If she discovered Principal R's whereabouts some-where on Maze Island!

She hurried over to the banks of the Once Upon River. Malorette and Odette were already waiting for her in one of the swan-shaped boats docked there. "I was beginning to wonder if you'd show up," said Malorette. She seemed impatient to be off.

"Got here as fast as I could," said Goldie, climbing inside the boat, too. "A jackrabbit guard stopped me on the drawbridge."

Odette rolled her eyes. "Yeah, those guards are crawling, hopping, and stomping all over the place these days." She didn't seem too happy about that, despite the fact that she and Malorette were always so admiring of Ms. Wicked.

"You guys can paddle," Malorette told Goldie, handing her and Odette each an oar. Then she settled back to let them do all the work. Goldie hoped Malorette hadn't invited her along just to help row. Though a bit suspicious about why the two sisters wanted to hang with her, she decided to go with the flow — literally *and* figuratively since they were now drifting down the river. If this truly was an offer of friendship, she didn't want to ruin it. Still, she did wonder why these girls had waited till now to befriend her when she'd already been at the Academy for three months.

As Goldie and Odette dipped and pulled on their paddles, Malorette relaxed on the seat beside her sister. Up on the towers, they could see various guards, some with spyglasses directed toward them.

Malorette glared at the guards and stuck out her tongue. "Stop it," said Odette. "Are you trying to get us locked in the dungeon?"

"They wouldn't dare," said Malorette. But she didn't

look completely sure about that. As Goldie had sensed, the sisters weren't exactly onboard with the recent changes. Still, she was surprised to hear them grumble about Ms. Wicked in front of her.

"You're just mad because she made you give up your skeleton key," Odette told her sister.

"You had a skeleton key?" Goldie asked Malorette, wide-eyed. A skeleton key was essentially a master key and was much easier to use than a hairpin in unlocking all kinds of doors. Goldie sort of thought that was cheating and prided herself on not needing such a key. She used her *skill* to open locks.

Malorette and Odette exchanged a hooded look. "It was for . . . um . . . trunker checks," Malorette volunteered.

"To make sure no one was keeping anything in their trunkers that they shouldn't," added Odette.

"Oh," said Goldie. "So you guys did trunker checks?"

"Somebody had to," said Odette, as if that were obvious.

The girls exchanged another secretive look. "Artifacts were going missing from the library for a while," Malorette informed her. "That's all we can say."

Pulling her paddle out of the water for a moment, Goldie watched the river glide by as their boat sliced through the water. She had a feeling that the sisters weren't quite telling the truth about those "trunker checks" — or not the whole of it, anyway — but she didn't call them on it.

Malorette turned toward Odette. "It isn't fair. We shouldn't be treated the same as other students. It's as if Ms. Wicked has decided not to trust us."

"Or that she's better than us now," said Odette.

"So you guys have, like, a special relationship with Ms. Wicked?" Goldie asked, curious.

"Naturally," Odette sniffed in a hoity-toity way. "We're all members of the E.V.I.L. Society."

"*Huh?*" Goldie was so startled at this frank admission that she dropped her oar. Who just came right out and admitted being evil as if it was nothing? Odette, apparently. Luckily, Goldie caught her paddle before it could be swept away by the river. She'd known that the two sisters were the "bad" characters in Cinderella's fairy tale, but she *hadn't* known they were members of E.V.I.L.!

"But the E.V.I.L. Society is a bad thing, right?" she blurted out. "*Evil*, just like their name. Principal R warned us about the group, and —"

"Whatever," Malorette interrupted, rolling her eyes. "You really shouldn't believe everything you hear. E.V.I.L. merely stands for **E**xceptional **V**illains **i**n **L**iterature."

"Yeah," said Goldie. "I know. *Villains.*"

"Well, then," said Odette. The two sisters eyed her appraisingly.

"Well, then what?" Goldie asked in confusion.

"We know your tale," Malorette said slowly, as if Goldie were a half-wit. "And we've decided you are a good fit. So we want to invite you to join!"

They grinned at her as though she was supposed to jump up in the boat right then and there and do a happy dance. But even if she'd felt inclined to do that — which she certainly did not — she wouldn't have risked tipping over the boat and spilling them all into the water.

"I am *not* a villain," she said, slapping her oar in the water for emphasis. "I mean, yes, I do let myself into an empty house in my tale. But I don't steal anything."

The sisters arched their eyebrows. "Hello? Bowls of porridge?" Odette said.

"Helping yourself to food when you're hungry is not the same thing as stealing," Goldie insisted.

"And you do break a chair," Malorette added. "That's *vandalism.*"

"Entirely accidental," Goldie protested hotly. "I don't do it on purpose!"

"Okay, okay, calm down," said Malorette. By now, the three girls had reached the shore of Maze Island. They hopped out and got busy pulling their boat onto the sandy beach. At least, Goldie got busy doing that. After one or two tugs, the other girls just left the work to her.

"What are we doing here, anyway?" Goldie asked once the job was done.

"You'll see," said Malorette. After grabbing a bag she'd stashed under her seat in the boat, she led the other two girls into the extensive hedge maze for which the island had been named. As they threaded their way through the twists and turns of the greenery, Goldie eyed the neatly trimmed hedges cut into various topiary shapes. Some resembled serpents or dragons, others malevolent-looking cats, growling dogs, or fantastical animals about to pounce.

"Cool, huh?" said Odette as they passed a topiary lion with an arched back and extended claws. "The island's looking really great, thanks to Principal W. She's been sprucing things up now that she's in charge."

"Thanks to who? Oh, you mean Ms. Wicked? She's only the *acting* principal," Goldie put in. "And I think topiaries are kind of creepy!" When the two sisters shared a frown, she immediately wished she could call back her words. Even if she did think the topiary was just another example of Ms. Wicked wanting to control things, she should have agreed with them. After all, she wanted them to like her. *Too late!*

Since the sisters knew their way, it didn't take long to reach the gazebo at the very center of the maze. It resembled a giant round, domed birdcage, with benches ringing the inside of it, and a life-size bronze statue of Principal R on a pedestal at the very middle.

Amidst Ms. Wicked's new and perfectly groomed changes, the old statue struck Goldie as oddly comforting.

Malorette opened the bag she'd brought with her and pulled out a tape measure. "Help me measure the pedestal, okay?" she said to Goldie, handing her one end of the tape.

"Uh, okay," said Goldie. She held on to her end while Malorette stretched the tape across one side of the statue's square base. "Twenty-four inches on a side," she reported.

"Got it," said Odette. She jotted down the measurement on a pad of paper she pulled from the pocket of her gown, along with a pencil.

"See these slightly melted places down here?" Malorette asked Goldie, drawing her attention to the base of the statue. "An alchemy accident."

"Yeah," Odette chuckled. "Principal Rumpeltwit and Ms. Jabberwocky were always trying to turn stuff to gold. Even his own statue. So lame."

"Let's measure the height of the statue next," said Malorette.

Goldie kept her end of the tape at the base while Malorette stretched her end to the tip-top of the bronze statue's tall hat. "Thirty-five inches," she reported to Odette, who scribbled down the number.

She looked at Goldie, then gestured up at the gazebo's barred wrought iron ceiling. "I'll hold my end of the tape down here. You shinny up and check how much room there is to make the statue taller," she suggested.

Before Goldie could ask if the statue was to be repaired and why Ms. Wicked would want to enlarge it rather than leave it life-size, Malorette gave her a boost up.

"Whoa!" said Goldie. Quickly, she grabbed on and climbed up the statue till she stood on the principal's shoulders. Clinging to a hanging flowerpot, she managed to measure the space available above Principal R's head. Calling out another dimension that Odette recorded dutifully, she started to shimmy down again. But then she looked out over the maze.

From here she could see the island's shore on all sides of them. And she saw at a glance that there weren't any cottages around. Which meant that those three bear guards couldn't be living here. How disappointing!

When Goldie's feet hit the ground a minute later, the two sisters were eyeing her sympathetically. Had they noticed her disappointment and figured out the reason for it?

"I bet you've been made to feel bad about being villainous all your life, haven't you?" Malorette surprised her by saying.

Goldie scrunched her nose, considering. *Have I?* she wondered. "I–I'm not sure about that." It was true her aunt had denied her many pleasures growing up, but she'd never said it was because Goldie was *villainous*.

"You may not realize it, but the so-called *good* characters in fairy tales look down on us," Malorette added, as she began to wind up the measuring tape.

"They do?" Goldie said. While she hadn't yet made a ton of friends at GA, no one had been awful to her. Was it possible that they really did look down on her? What a grimmorrible thought!

Odette slipped her pad of paper and pencil back into her pocket. "Don't worry. With Principal W in charge, that's going to change!" she crowed.

"But are you sure it will be a change for the better?" Goldie asked in earnest. "You said it yourselves. *All* of us students have fewer liberties now than ever before, with Ms. Wicked in charge."

Malorette frowned as she slipped the tape measure into her bag. "That's only temporary," she said.

"And it's for our own good," added Odette. Only she didn't sound as if she quite believed that herself.

Still, Goldie decided not to push things. Malorette and Odette seemed to be genuinely offering her their friendship. Although she wasn't sure if they truly liked her or just wanted her to join a Society she'd really rather not have anything to do with, she was not about to nip their offer in the bud. So she would *not* indulge in her usual bad habit of saying exactly what she thought. Which was that the security changes were only for Ms. Wicked's own good!

"So I guess Ms. Wicked plans to repair the alchemy damage to Principal R's statue, huh?" Goldie said as the three girls started back through the maze. "That's why we were taking measurements?"

"What? No way!" said Malorette. "She's going to have that old statue torn down so she can erect one of herself in its place."

A cold chill ran down Goldie's spine. "But what about when Principal R returns?" she asked levelly.

"Oh, he probably won't be back," Malorette said, exchanging a sly smile with her sister.

"What? Why do you say that?" Goldie asked.

"Just a hunch," said Odette. The girls grinned at each other, sending another chill down Goldie's spine. She recalled what she'd overheard them saying in their dorm room yesterday about the principal's fate being sealed and wondered exactly how much they knew.

"Do you know where he is?" she asked point blankly. "Or why Ms. Wicked called a halt to his straw-into-gold spinning trials? I mean, if the Academy needs money, it seems like she'd want to continue them."

Both girls shrugged. "No clue," said Odette. "But in my opinion, those trials were pointless. That straw is a dud. Everyone who has tried spinning it says so."

They exited the maze just as another swan boat landed on the shore. Three animal guards — the same beaver Goldie had seen outside the Great Hall at lunch, plus two more beavers — climbed out of the boat. Each had a sledge-hammer lifted to its shoulder. Dressed in their navy blue uniforms and walking upright on two legs, they came up to the girls.

"Principal W said we'd find you here," said the pencil-chewing beaver from lunch. His words whistled through his large top and bottom teeth, and his broad tail slapped the ground. "We're the demolition crew. Now, where's that statue we're supposed to take down?"

Malorette pointed over her shoulder. "At the center of the maze. If you need help finding —" Abruptly, she stopped speaking. The three beavers had already taken off! She glanced at Odette meaningfully. "Talk about eager beavers!" she said with a laugh as the girls climbed back into their boat.

Odette grinned at her sister and recited, "The big bad eager beavers bit the bigger, better badgers." She looked over at Goldie. "I made that tongue twister up for Enchantments class when we grew those plants for the festival, remember? What did you grow on yours?"

Goldie stared at her as they both used the oars to push off from shore. "Furry foxes and fuzzy bears. So those beaver guards we just saw . . . and the others . . ."

"Just worked that out, did you?" Malorette said, sounding amused. "Yes. Clever of Principal W to save the magic blossoms from all of our tongue twister plants and magic them into a security force for the Academy, huh?"

"Um, yeah," Goldie muttered. So she'd guessed right about that. It was alarming to have her guess confirmed. She needed to talk about this to someone. But who? Not these girls.

On the trip back across the river, Malorette produced some yummy-looking three-dimensional gingerbread house cookies from her bag.

"Snack?" she asked, holding a cookie out to Goldie. The cookies were one of Mistress Hagscorch's specialties. They were beautifully decorated with candies and icing, each just big enough to fit in the palm of one hand.

"Snitched goodies always taste better than those given freely, don't you think?" Odette commented when Goldie was already half finished with her cookie.

"Mmfh?" Goldie mumbled around a mouthful of cookie.

"Don't look so shocked," Malorette said, giggling at her expression. "Yeah, I snitched them from the kitchen without permission. C'mon. It's not like you haven't done the same thing. Your tale, remember? Eating someone else's porridge? Same as stealing if you're being honest with yourself." Then she added, "No judgment, though."

As if that was supposed to reassure her? Goldie hurriedly finished off the cookie, anyway, and then tried to forget about it.

Pushed along by the current, it was an easy paddle back to the Academy. Odette was first to leap out of the boat as soon as they docked. "Gotta run. See you," she told Goldie.

"Yeah," said Malorette. "After we deliver these measurements to Principal W, we have to study. Grimm History of Barbarians and Dastardlies test tomorrow!"

"Oh, yeah. Me too," said Goldie.

Malorette winked at Goldie. "Even *bad* villains can be *good* students, right?" Both sisters giggled as they dashed off.

Goldie couldn't help grinning, too. Malorette and Odette weren't *all* bad. If she joined E.V.I.L., she'd probably make other friends. All of them villains. But the Grimm brothers had invited good *and* bad fairy-tale characters into Grimmlandia. They hadn't seen any reason to exclude the bad ones. Could good not exist without bad around? At least in fairy tales? She supposed that made some kind of sense.

6

The Dungeon

A few minutes later, Goldie pushed back the curtain door to her shared alcove in Ruby Tower. She saw right away that Polly had a visitor. Jill, who was also a nursery rhyme character, attended the Academy with her brother, Jack. She was sitting on the rug next to Polly, and both girls were sipping tea. *Tea for two,* Goldie thought with a smile.

The girls were chatting and laughing in the close, familiar way Goldie had observed between best friends. She had yet to experience this herself, since she'd never had a best friend. A bolt of jealousy slipped through her, but she pushed it away. She was glad *somebody* around here had friends!

Seeing Goldie, Jill jumped up. "Hi!" Then to Polly, she added, "Better run."

"No need to go just because I'm here," Goldie joked. "I mean, where's the fire?" She'd added that last part because

Jack and Jill actually had a magic fire pail they used for putting out fires around the Academy. But no one laughed.

"Uh, no fire," said Jill, who either didn't get Goldie's joke or just didn't think it was funny. "I've got a lot of stuff to do, that's all." She glanced over at Polly, who was drinking probably her bazillionth cup of tea for the day. "See you at dinner." Then she whisked out through the curtain.

"Want some?" Polly, asked, pointing to a china teapot that sat beside her on the rug. "It's herbal," she added. "I never drink caffeine after two in the afternoon. Otherwise I can't sleep."

"Sure, I'll have a cup," Goldie said, relieved that Polly seemed her usual tea-obsessed self and not mad at her for what had happened at breakfast.

"What were you guys talking about?" she asked Polly.

"Oh, you know, just stuff," said Polly, shrugging.

Hmph! Not just tea then, Goldie guessed. Suddenly, a new, uncomfortable thought occurred to her. Maybe Polly didn't trust her. Maybe she considered her a porridge thief and a chair vandalizer, too. Maybe she thought Goldie would fit right in with E.V.I.L. Did she talk about tea so much around her only because it seemed a safe subject? It was a hurtful thought, but it was possible. Distrust among students had grown a lot since Ms. Wicked had become principal.

"Thanks," Goldie said, taking a seat on the rug as Polly poured and then handed her a cup. "Mmm," she said, after taking a sip. "Usually peppermint is not my cup of tea," she joked, "but this is delish. Not too hot and not too cold. It's just right."

Polly smiled. "So how was your trip to Maze Island?"

"Okay." Goldie was hesitant to talk about that since Malorette and Odette's room was right next door. They might overhear. "How were your classes today?" she asked instead, determined to talk about something other than tea for once.

"Okay," said Polly. She topped off the tea in her cup, then after a moment's hesitation, she added, "A rumor about Principal R was going around during my sixth-period Calligraphy and Illuminated Manuscripts class."

Goldie raised an eyebrow. "Oh?"

"That he's being kept in the Pink Castle dungeon."

"What?" Goldie asked skeptically. "If he really is down there, it seems like someone would have discovered him by now. And who would lock him up?" she asked, curious to hear Polly's response.

"There are lots of ideas about that," her roomie said. Then she ticked off a list of people and groups the students in her class thought could have a reason for locking up Principal R. The list included the School Board, angry townspeople, E.V.I.L., malicious fairies, and even Grandmother Enchantress, Grimmlandia's most ancient and revered magical resident!

"Interesting. And creepy. Just imagine if he really is imprisoned down there. He'd be right under our noses. Or more like about six floors or so under our *feet*." Goldie shivered. As far-fetched as the idea that Principal R could be imprisoned beneath Pink Castle sounded to her, Malorette and Odette had seemed pretty sure he wouldn't be returning to GA. If she went down there and freed him, she'd be an instant hero. Well, to everyone but E.V.I.L.

Polly shivered, too. "I don't want to imagine it. Let's hit the books. History test tomorrow."

Goldie nodded, but she shot Polly a glance as both girls sat down at their desks. She wanted to ask her what she knew about E.V.I.L. and its members, but she wasn't sure how to bring up the topic. Did she know Malorette and Odette were members of the E.V.I.L. Society? If so, did she think the two sisters' friendliness with her signaled that she was a member, too? It was true they'd invited her to join the Society, but she hadn't said yes!

At eight o'clock that night, after most students had finished dinner and retired to their rooms, Goldie secretly slipped from Ruby Tower and down the stairs to the basement. It wouldn't hurt to check out the rumor about the principal being in the dungeon. Only she'd decided to do it *before* curfew this time. Less risky that way. There was no rule she knew of — either in the Handbook or from the lips of Ms. Wicked — that forbade students from going down to the very bottom of the castle. Of course, picking the locks on any locked doors she happened to encounter was another matter, but that couldn't be helped.

Animal guards were stationed at each landing she came to, but she told them she was looking for the Grimmstone Library in order to meet friends and study for a test. This satisfied them all and they let her pass by with warnings to be back in her dorm before ten.

Goldie had no valid reason for going down to the basement, however, since the library never appeared there, as far as she knew. So when she reached the first-floor landing, she said to the kangaroo guard stationed there, "The big bear guard is looking for you."

"Really?" The kangaroo guard hopped up and down anxiously. "Where is he?"

"Way up on the sixth floor," fibbed Goldie, pointing a finger upward.

Boing! Without another word, the kangaroo leaped past her to bound upstairs. Goldie thanked her lucky stars the guard was gullible enough to fall for her trick. "Though come to think of it," she mumbled to herself, "how bright could a blossom-turned-guard be?"

As soon as the kangaroo disappeared from sight, she ran down the last flight of stairs to the basement landing. There she came upon a narrow black door with big iron hinges. Naturally, it was locked. So she slipped the pearl-flower hairpin from her golden curls and stuck it in the lock. As she fumbled around, feeling for the just right place to poke, she heard footsteps coming downstairs behind her.

She darted glances over her shoulder, starting to panic in earnest. *Click!* Finally! The lock gave way.

Breathing a sigh of relief, she shoved open the door. After stepping quickly through, she softly closed the door behind her. The air was chilly and dank as she hurried through a long, sloping tunnel paved with cobblestones. Fortunately, antique brass lamps stuck out from the tunnel walls every few feet, lighting her way as she ventured deep beneath the castle. At last, at the end of the tunnel, she came upon a heavy iron door with a barred window in it. *Aha! A prison cell!*

Was Principal R inside? Her heart thumped with excitement. She felt sure she was *this* close to setting him free and becoming the school hero!

She was startled to hear muffled voices coming from beyond the door. It sounded like more than one person was locked up in the cell. Standing on tiptoe, she peeked through the barred window.

To her great disappointment, Principal R was not inside. Instead, she saw a regular bedroom. And two girls she knew — Rapunzel and Red Riding Hood — were sitting and chatting on top of a bed covered in a black duvet. *Bummer and a half!* Her hopes of heroism were instantly dashed.

There were several cats in the room as well. Rapunzel was petting a black one. Two more black cats were curled up together at the end of the bed, while a fluffy gray cat paced on a black-and-white-checkered rug nearby. And there was an all-white cat sitting on top of a black-painted desk, licking its paws.

Goldie loved animals, but her aunt had never allowed her to have a pet. "They're dirty, messy creatures," she'd always said. Which wasn't true *or* fair, but her aunt had very definite opinions about things. And arguing with her had never done Goldie any good and had only seemed to make her aunt more certain she was right.

Goldie was so entranced by the cats that she failed to notice someone had followed her down the tunnel. And she didn't hear the soft footsteps coming up behind her. But when she felt a tap on her shoulder, she let out a shriek. *"Eek!"* She wheeled around.

"Shh. It's just me," said Polly. "I saw you leave Ruby Tower and followed you to find out what you were up to." She craned her head toward the barred window. "Did you find him? Is Principal R in there?"

Before Goldie could reply, the door was thrust open.

"Goldie?" Rapunzel's dark eyes went wide in surprise.

"Polly?" said Red. She and Rapunzel looked from one girl to the other. "What are you two doing here?" they chorused.

"I — that is — *we*," Goldie stuttered, gesturing toward Polly, "were looking for Principal R."

"Well, this is my room and he's not in here," Rapunzel said emphatically. "And you're not the first to come down to this dungeon looking for him. We've heard the rumors, too, but they're false."

Soon, all four girls were comfortably seated on Rapunzel's black-and-white-checkered rug, leaning against tasseled black-and-white pillows of various shapes and sizes. A white cat leaped down from Rapunzel's desk and ran over to Goldie, her tail waving high in the air.

"Moon likes you," Rapunzel informed Goldie.

Well, that makes one for-sure friend, thought Goldie as

she petted the cat. Moon stretched out on her legs and began to purr.

"So if Principal R isn't down here, where do we think he is?" Polly asked, looking around at Goldie, Red, and Rapunzel.

"No clue," Rapunzel answered, stroking her fluffy gray cat under its chin. "Wherever he is, I hope he's okay. I mean, he was really nice to me. I was kind of afraid of heights plus I needed somewhere big to keep all my cats, so he gave me permission to choose a room down here in the dungeon. But now I'm starting to worry that Ms. Wicked will remember I'm where I am and make me move to one of the towers."

"For your own safety," Red said, imitating Ms. Wicked's imperious voice.

All four girls laughed. It was easy to see why Red had starred in a school play. She had Ms. Wicked's voice and manner down perfectly!

Goldie glanced around, taking in more of Rapunzel's dungeon room. It was really adorable — in a goth kind of way. Black lacy curtains hung from a second barred window above the bed. "So you really live here?" she asked finally.

Rapunzel nodded, as her fluffy gray cat pushed its big head under her hand.

"Yeah, she did it up cute, right? She even made that awesome mural herself," said Red. She waved toward a stone wall painted with a nighttime forest scene. In various shades of black, silver, white, and other dusky colors, bats and owls flitted through a moonlit sky while heavy-limbed trees swayed below them.

"Grimmazing!" Goldie pronounced in admiring tones.

Suddenly Rapunzel cocked her head, like she was trying to figure something out. "You know what's weird, though? I just remembered I locked the tunnel door when Red and I came down here after dinner. So how did you guys get in just now?"

Polly shrugged. "We didn't come together. I followed Goldie. And when I got to the door, it wasn't locked."

Everyone looked at Goldie.

"Um," she said. "The lock was broken."

"Really?" Rapunzel said in alarm. She hopped off the bed. "Let's go check it. I don't want guards or Ms. Wicked's spies creeping down here."

Seeing no good way around it, Goldie followed the other girls back down the hall toward the lock, dragging her feet. How was she going to explain this? She'd lied, for one thing. And she'd picked a lock — a big no-no — for another.

As they got closer and closer to the door, Goldie held

back even more. When the others found out the lock wasn't actually broken, maybe she could suggest the janitor must have repaired it right away. Only she knew how unlikely that would seem. She and Polly had just come through the door not long ago and there hadn't been enough time for the janitor to happen by, notice the lock was broken, and then fix it, too.

Besides, she didn't really want to get tangled up in yet another lie. When Rapunzel reached out to examine the lock, Goldie finally blurted out the truth. "Oh, all right. I picked it. I admit it."

"Picked what?" asked Red.

"The lock. It's not broken. I used this." Goldie slid the pearl-flower pin from her hair and handed it to Rapunzel to pass around.

"Whoa, how grimmtastic is that? Wish I had the skill to pick locks," Rapunzel exclaimed. She studied the pin in admiration then passed it to Red.

"You're not mad?" asked Goldie. "You guys don't think I'm a villain? Because I think you can be a *good* character in a fairy tale without actually being *goody-goody*."

"Huh?" asked Polly. The girls stared at her, obviously confused.

"Oh, never mind," said Goldie, deciding to leave well enough alone.

"It's pretty," Polly said when it was her turn to look at the pin. "A gift from your aunt?"

"Uh, not quite," Goldie told her, thinking there was no way her aunt would ever give her something so pretty and . . . *ornamental.* "I discovered it on the top shelf of my trunker a couple of weeks ago. I guess it must have been there all along and I just missed seeing it. Probably left there by the last student assigned to my trunker."

"Maybe," said Polly, handing the pin back to Goldie, who slid it into her hair. But she had sounded doubtful. From the corner of her eye, Goldie noticed her exchange a look with Red and Rapunzel. *What was that all about?* she wondered.

Just then, they heard a sound. *Boing! Boing!*

"Uh-oh! The kangaroo guard," hissed Goldie. "Quick! Relock the door."

Red was closest, so she did. Just in time! Right away, the doorknob rattled. The four girls backed away, then took off running, not stopping till they were in Rapunzel's room again. Red and Rapunzel flopped onto the bed, gasping after their quick escape. Goldie and Polly flopped onto the rug.

"To get rid of that kangaroo before I went down to the basement, I told him another guard was looking for him," said Goldie, still panting. "Bet he was hopping mad when he found out otherwise."

For some reason, this made everyone giddy and they all started laughing. When they finally calmed down, Goldie told the others what she'd learned about the guards having sprung from tongue twister plants.

Rapunzel and Red sat up on the bed and nodded. "Yeah! We figured out the same thing," said Red.

"My tongue twister was 'Zany Zachary zigzagged alone through the zoo's zebra zone with his xylophone,'" said Rapunzel.

Everyone giggled, reciting their tongue twisters, too. "Mine was 'Five fuzzy bears followed four furry foxes in the forest,'" said Goldie. Moon had fallen asleep on top of her. Trying not to disturb the cat, she lay as still as she could with her legs stretched out before her.

"The bear and the fox guards, right?" Polly said from beside her. "Only aren't there just *three* bear guards?"

Goldie explained about the two unmagicked bear blossoms that sat on her desk.

"Oh, yeah, I've seen them. Cute!" said Polly.

Despite Malorette and Odette's assertion that the "so-called good" characters looked down on the villainous ones, Goldie thought Rapunzel and Red — and Polly, too, of course — were really very nice.

After a brief hesitation, she set Moon aside so she could sit up straight. Then she began to spill more of the things she'd learned that day. "Ms. Wicked is having the statue of Principal R in the Maze Island gazebo replaced with one of herself," she shared.

"What?" exclaimed Red.

Goldie nodded. "It's true. Malorette and Odette went there to measure the height from the base to the gazebo's ceiling to see how tall the new statue could be. And when I protested that Ms. Wicked was only the *acting* principal and asked what about Principal R, they just smiled. Then Malorette said, '*Oh, he probably won't be back.*' Odette said it was just their hunch, but I think they know more than they let on."

"Well, *my* hunch is that E.V.I.L. has Principal R in its clutches," said Polly.

Red nodded. "It wouldn't surprise me."

"Ditto." Rapunzel's long, loose braids, which hung nearly to the floor, bobbed up and down as she nodded, too.

"Too bad we don't have proof of that, though," said Red. She looked at Goldie. "You know Snow White? Well, she was a member of E.V.I.L. for a while, and —"

"She was?" Polly interrupted, eyes wide.

"Only so she could spy on them," Red hastened to add. "She wasn't ever really evil but only convinced Ms. Wicked — her stepmother, that is — that she was on E.V.I.L.'s side."

"Ms. Wicked wasn't fooled for long," said Rapunzel, taking up the thread of the story as she got up and went over to the window to let one of her cats outside. "So then, Snow used her magic charm tiara, which allows her to become invisible, to spy on the society."

Wow, thought Goldie. *Snow's magic charm tiara can make her invisible? How cool is that?* She'd learned about magic charms during her first week at the Academy. Red and Rapunzel and certain other students had them. It was an honor to be chosen by a charm, and most students went to GA for months or years before it happened. Charms had magical powers that only the person they belonged to could unlock.

Goldie went to stand by Rapunzel at the window to watch her cat scamper off toward the river. But her attention snapped back to the group when Red took over the story again. "Spying on E.V.I.L. while she was invisible worked for Snow for a while," she said. "But then the Society got suspicious. They began cloaking their meetings with a magic spell to prevent outsiders — even *invisible* outsiders — from getting in to spy."

By now, Goldie's mind was spinning. She twisted a lock of golden hair around her finger. "I could get in to spy on E.V.I.L.!" she blurted to the others. "Malorette and Odette invited me to join."

The other three girls stared at her in surprise. And maybe a hint of sudden suspicion.

"Why?" asked Polly.

"They think I'm evil because of some stuff in my tale, but I'm not. Promise." Goldie drew and invisible *X* on her chest with a fingertip, crossing her heart. "I'm on your side. And I'm pretty positive they don't know where Principal R is being kept, but Ms. Wicked has *got* to know." Her eyes shone bright. "If I join the Society, maybe I can get her to tell me where he is." Spying on E.V.I.L. was sure to make her a hero! Especially if it helped her find the principal.

The other three girls were silent for a moment, as they considered what she'd said. Finally, Red rose to her feet and began to pace to and fro. "You'll have to be very, very careful," she cautioned. "Ms. Wicked isn't easy to deceive. Even Snow, her own stepdaughter, couldn't fool her forever."

"And she's not the only teacher who's a Society member, by the way," said Rapunzel. "Ms. Queenharts is, too."

"Really?" chorused Goldie and Polly. The snobbish Ms. Queenharts taught Comportment, which basically dealt with the subject of etiquette or good manners.

Red and Rapunzel nodded. "And Mr. Hump-Dumpty was a member at one time, too," said Rapunzel.

"But as far as we know, he's since dropped out of the group," added Red.

The egg-shaped Mr. Hump-Dumpty taught the Grimm History of Barbarians and Dastardlies. Goldie had always thought him a good egg, so it surprised her that he'd ever been a member. He was always very fearful, though, so maybe he'd been scared into joining?

"The only student members we're sure about are Malorette and Odette," said Rapunzel, moving from the window to sit cross-legged on her bed. "E.V.I.L. members wear masks to meetings, or at least they used to. Which means that even if you do succeed in getting in, it may be tricky to figure out who's who."

"Another thing — Ms. Wicked knows we're good characters and can't be swayed into joining the Society for real. So if you *do* join, you'll need to keep our friendship a secret," Red added.

Their *friendship*? So Red considered them *friends* now? Goldie beamed at her. "Oh! No problem." *Woo-hoo!* She wanted to jump for joy. These non-evil girls were starting to like her!

Rapunzel nodded. "It's lucky that you and Polly are roommates. You can tell her whatever you find out in the secrecy of your room. And then she can report back to us."

"Tea-tastic idea," said Polly. Which made the others smile.

"We'll share whatever you tell Polly and Polly tells us with Snow and Cinda, of course," Red added. "Even though Cinda is Malorette and Odette's stepsister, she's not at all like them. And she's certainly no fan of E.V.I.L."

"Okay," Goldie agreed. Cinda, she knew, was the *good* character in the tale she shared with her two villainous stepsisters. She, Snow, Red, and Rapunzel were all best friends. If Goldie could make her friendship stick with these three girls, it might spread to include Cinda and Snow!

"And if Goldie can find out where Principal R is being kept, we'll make a plan to rescue him?" Polly asked.

Goldie nodded along with the others. But at the same time, she was thinking that if anyone was going to make and carry out a plan to rescue the principal, it was going to be *her*!

When it came time to leave Rapunzel's dungeon room, the girls all decided that Goldie should go on ahead of Red and Polly so that no one would see them together. "Malorette and Odette would drop you like a hot potato if they thought you were friendly with us *good* characters," Rapunzel warned. "And then there'd be no chance of your getting into E.V.I.L."

Though it hurt a little to think that Malorette and Odette's offer of friendship was so fragile, Goldie didn't doubt that Rapunzel was right. If she did become a member of that Society, she'd have to keep her wits about her. A broken friendship would probably be the least of her worries if Malorette and Odette and other members of E.V.I.L. were to find out what she was up to!

7

Safe and Secure

"So?" said Malorette.

Goldie jumped about a mile high. Still half-asleep, she hadn't noticed Malorette and Odette were waiting outside her alcove as she left it to go down to breakfast the next morning.

"Oh! You scared me," she told them. For a moment she worried that they might've somehow found out about her dungeon wanderings last night and were going to confront her about where she'd been and with who.

However, as the three of them started down the stairs together, Malorette brought up another subject entirely. "So you never did say if you were interested in joining our *group*. We're recruiting new members and we'd be willing to sponsor you," she said.

"*Sponsor* me? What does that mean exactly?" Goldie had been a little afraid the sisters would take back their invitation to join the Society since she'd been less than enthusiastic about membership yesterday. She was glad the offer was still on the table, but she didn't want to appear too eager.

"It means we suggested your name to Principal Wicked yesterday," said Odette. "So if you *are* interested, we'll take you to a screening interview in her office at lunchtime."

"I didn't know it was that hard to get in. Who else is in the Society, anyway?" Goldie asked, carefully keeping her voice casual. It would be great if she could get them to tell her a few names right off the bat.

Malorette shook her head as the girls entered the Great Hall. "That's strictly on a need-to-know basis. First, there are rules. Steps."

"Ms. Wicked has to approve you for membership, and then there's a probationary period," Odette explained as they headed for the breakfast line.

"Wow," said Goldie. "Quite a process."

"Yes, well, we don't let just anyone in, you know. There have been a few . . . *problems* in the past," Malorette told her. She glanced in the direction of Snow White, who was just passing them with her breakfast tray on the way to sit with her besties — Rapunzel, Red, and Cinda.

A little thrill shot through Goldie to think that those four girls were quite possibly on their way to becoming *her* friends, too. She was careful to avoid making eye contact with any of them, though. She didn't want Malorette and Odette to suspect anything. It was actually kind of dizzying going from hardly any friends at all to sudden offers of friendship from both good and bad students.

Odette stared at Goldie as they took trays and got into the breakfast line. "Well?" she coaxed. "Do you want to meet for an interview at lunchtime or not?"

"Um . . . sure . . . why not?" said Goldie. Then, worried she hadn't sounded eager enough, she added, "I'd love to find out more. It would be grimmawesome or should I say *grimmevil* to become part of the group."

Choosing the right level of enthusiasm was tricky. She wanted her interest in joining E.V.I.L. to appear not too lukewarm, not too eager, but just right. She must've been convincing because Odette and Malorette both sent her pleased smiles as they split off for breakfast.

During first-period History, Goldie was so anxious about what questions Ms. Wicked might ask in the upcoming interview, that she was pretty sure she didn't do well on her test. By the time she entered Ms. Blue's Bespellings and Enchantments classroom third period, she felt super stressed. It didn't help that a uniformed zebra guard was trotting back and forth at the rear of the classroom, eyeing students through tinted glasses with black-and-white-striped frames.

Huh? thought Goldie. Till now, the guards had only patrolled *outside* the classrooms. This was something new. And it made her feel even more jittery.

However, her apprehension melted some when Prince Foulsmell caught her gaze. He nodded toward the guard and rolled his eyes, then smiled at her. She rolled her eyes and smiled back.

Ms. Blue tapped her wand and made an announcement right away. "Today we'll begin creating magic projects as part of a celebration to dedicate a new statue of Principal Wicked. The statue will be erected out on Maze Island in the coming weeks." Her voice sounded a bit too bright to Goldie, as if she were forcing herself to sound enthusiastic.

Celebratory projects? An exploding cake that splatted frosting on Ms. Wicked's face sounded just perfect for the occasion to Goldie, but she doubted it would be wise to suggest such a project idea with that zebra guard around.

Foulsmell raised his hand. "Aren't we going to continue with the Defensive Magic unit we started yesterday?" he asked when he was called on.

Ms. Blue glanced nervously at the zebra guard. It

lowered its striped tinted glasses to glare at Foulsmell. "Zzuch zzpells are not needed zzince all izz zzafe and zzecure now," it said.

Hmph, thought Goldie. She and Foulsmell exchanged disappointed glances. Murmurs swept the class. They weren't the only disappointed ones. Those bubbles had been fun!

"You'll find some spells to help you get ideas in Chapter Eleven of your Handbooks," Ms. Blue said quickly.

What? thought Goldie. Yesterday, Chapter Eleven had been the chapter on Defensive Magic. But when she asked her Handbook to magically open itself to that chapter now, she saw that its heading read "Decorative Magic" instead. *What was going on?* She checked the Table of Contents, in case she'd remembered wrong. There was no "Defensive Magic" chapter anymore! Returning to Chapter Eleven, she skimmed the first paragraph:

Celebrations of all kinds can be made a lot more fun with magic. From displays that sparkle and light up the sky, to party decorations that can actually move and talk, to amazing foods that tickle the tongue, this chapter provides you with all the spells you will need to ensure that your special occasion — or the occasion of a very special, very, very important person at your school perhaps — is not just special, but magically, sensationally special!

She leaned across the table to speak to Mermily, who was also staring at her Handbook. "Something's up," Goldie said. "This chapter used to be . . ." She zipped her lip when the zebra guard, who'd been keeping a keen eye on Ms. Blue and all of the students, trotted up to her.

"Izz there a problem?" it asked.

"No." Goldie sent the guard a fake smile and stared back at her book as though it were the most fascinating chapter she'd ever laid eyes on. She couldn't do anything that might raise the zebra guard's suspicion of her, she realized. If it reported to Ms. Wicked against her, her plans to gather information from E.V.I.L. would be foiled!

Asking Ms. Blue about the chapter was out of the question, as well. That guard was watching their every move and seemed to be making the teacher as nervous as the rest of them. So instead, Goldie spent the period practicing a dumb spell to create party streamers of various colors that shot up from the tip of her wand to drape themselves in the air. *Zzzo boring!*

"Hey, Goldie, wait up!" Prince Foulsmell called as they exited class at the end of the period. Out in the hall she was about to drop back and see what he wanted, when Malorette and Odette appeared to escort her to her interview with Ms. Wicked. When Foulsmell caught up to her, the two sisters got in his way, elbowing him aside. Linking arms with her, they steered Goldie down the hall toward the grand staircase that would take them up to the principal's office on the fourth floor.

Noting that Foulsmell had followed them, Malorette made a face. "I warned you about that puppy-dog prince, didn't I?" she asked Goldie, not even trying to keep her voice down.

"You weren't going to hang out with him, were you?" Odette chided her as Foulsmell trailed them. Before Goldie could think what to reply, Odette looked over her shoulder at the prince. "Woof, woof!" she barked at him.

Horrified by this rudeness, Goldie glanced back, too.

With a look of confusion on his face, the prince had halted in mid-stride.

The sisters didn't let up and also began to laugh. "Git along, little doggie!" Malorette called to him, making shooing motions with her hands.

An embarrassed flush was spreading up his neck to his cheeks. Foulsmell spun around and stalked off in the opposite direction down the hall. It had all happened so fast that Goldie could only watch, speechless with dismay. Instantly, a sick kind of feeling hit her. She could go after Foulsmell and explain, but that would foil her chances of getting into the Society. And foiling E.V.I.L. would be for the greater good of the whole school in the end. Surely Foulsmell would understand if she could tell him what was going on. Which she couldn't. Argh!

This totally stunk. What they'd done to Foulsmell had been awful, and had hurt his feelings. Not only that, he probably thought she had been making fun of him, too!

"Why were you so mean?" she asked the sisters as they climbed from the third to the fourth floor. "He's not a bad guy."

That set the sisters to laughing again. "Exactly," said Malorette. "Not *bad*. Which means he's not *our* type."

"Hope you're prepared for this interview," said Odette as they started down the fourth-floor hallway. "Because ours was grueling. Remember, Malorette?"

"Yeah. It was a total nightmare."

Goldie tensed. Worry about the interview suddenly trumped worry about Foulsmell's hurt feelings. "You didn't say anything about preparing. What was I supposed to —"

But they had already arrived at the office door. Her companions opened it and gave her a little push inside before following her in. She'd just have to field any questions that came her way the best she could. *Gulp!*

8

E.V.I.L. Interview

When the three girls entered the main office, they startled Ms. Jabberwocky, who was in the act of gulping down a hot pepper. A stream of flame shot from the dragon lady's nostrils, setting a stack of papers on her desk ablaze.

"Oh, frabjous, just frabjous. Not!" she muttered as she grabbed the papers and shook them up and down to put out the fire. In the process, she created a cloud of gray smoke that she quickly tried to fan away. The dragon lady's odd way of talking and her fondness for hot peppers (and hot sauce as well!) were well known to both students and staff at the Academy.

But not everyone liked it. In fact, within seconds, a scowling Ms. Wicked burst from the door beyond Ms. Jabberwocky's desk. Once marked as PRINCIPAL R'S OFFICE, it now sported a new brass plate engraved with the words PRINCIPAL WICKED.

"Didn't I tell you the Academy is now a smoke-free zone?" Ms. Wicked yelled at the hapless dragon-lady assistant. "Unless I direct you to fry something, you don't fry something! Got it? And if you must eat those disgusting peppers and drink that revolting hot sauce, do it on your breaks. At a distance of at least thirty feet from the wooden drawbridges!"

Ms. Jabberwocky cringed under the tirade. "I know, I know, Principal Wicked. I'm tulgey sorry."

"Hmph," said Ms. Wicked. Then, distracted by a small gilt-framed mirror hanging on the side of a filing cabinet nearby, she leaned toward it and began to primp. "There are lots of others who could do your job, you know," she said as she patted her hair into place. "No one is irreplaceable." Still scowling, she reached into her pocket, withdrew a lipgloss, and began to apply it.

Ms. Jabberwocky grinned impudently, displaying sharp, scary teeth. Imitating her new employer while her back was turned, she ran a clawed hand over the scales at the top of her head as if to smooth them to controlled perfection. Then she puckered her lips and smacked them together. Goldie had to clap a hand over her mouth to stifle a giggle. Luckily, Malorette and Odette didn't notice the dragon lady's mockery *or* Goldie's response. The two sisters had eyes only for Ms. Wicked.

When she finished primping and turned around again, Ms. Wicked finally noticed the three girls standing just inside the office door. Like magic, the scowl on her face vanished and was replaced by her usual charming, but icy, smile. "You should have told me my guests had arrived," she scolded Ms. Jabberwocky in a lighter tone. "But never mind. Come in, come in, girls."

She ushered them into the office that used to belong to Principal R. Goldie had been in it only once before, when she'd first arrived at Grimm Academy. She remembered then that it had been full of equipment and supplies related to the principal's alchemy experiments, including a large heavy-duty metal worktable. All that was gone now.

Also gone were the shelves on either side of the room that had held strangely shaped dark lumps that looked like bad art sculptures but were really just the charred remains of gold-making experiments gone wrong. There had been jars of gold-colored flakes on the shelves, a tank of swimming goldfish, and a vase of goldenrods. Goldie had especially liked a picture of a golden retriever. It had hung on the wall behind the principal's solid-gold throne, which bore the GA logo carved into its high back.

Except for the throne and Principal R's large desk, all of his things had been removed. Almost every inch of wall space was now hung with mirrors of various sizes and shapes, all in elaborately ornamented silver and gold frames. And there was a lovely antique marble-topped table at one end of the room. It was covered with food. Goldie started edging toward it. She couldn't help herself. She was starving!

Meanwhile, Ms. Wicked smiled at her many reflections, obviously pleased with the perfection she saw there. Then, with an effort, she tore her eyes away from the mirrors and gestured toward the lavish spread of breads, meats, fruits, vegetables, and sweets that sat upon the table. "Since I knew you'd be missing lunch, I had one of Mistress Hagscorch's helpers bring a little something up from the kitchen. Please, help yourself."

Goldie picked up a plate, her mouth watering. However, as she added a buttered roll to the mound of food she piled high on her plate, she wondered if Ms. Wicked were actually trying to butter *her* up for some reason by providing such a sumptuous banquet. The three girls sat in cushioned chairs around the table, with Goldie opposite Ms. Wicked.

While the girls ate, Ms. Wicked quickly got to the point. "Malorette and Odette have told me they think you're a good candidate for membership in the E.V.I.L. Society," she said to Goldie. "You've been here at the Academy for three months now. Correct?"

"Yerp, thas right," Goldie managed to say around a mouthful of ripe strawberries. If all of Ms. Wicked's questions were as easy to answer as that one, this interview would be a breeze. But, as it turned out, that was just wishful thinking.

Ms. Wicked gazed intently at her from across the food-laden table. "Tell me. Why do you want to be in E.V.I.L.?" she asked next. "Can you give me your reasons?"

"I . . . uh . . ." floundered Goldie. A bit of bread stuck in her throat and she swallowed hard. She could feel her face flush. She should have realized this was something Ms. Wicked would ask! As she struggled to come up with good and convincing reasons (lies, actually) for wanting to be a member of the Society, Ms. Wicked admired herself in the mirrors on the wall closest to the table.

"Take your time," she said, patting her hair again. Then she smiled a self-important smile. "But not *too* much time. My principal duties, added to my teaching responsibilities, have made me a very busy woman these days."

That's it! thought Goldie, straightening in her chair. She'd make up "reasons" that would appeal to Ms. Wicked's vanity and sense of importance. She leaned forward earnestly. "Yes, I can only imagine how busy you must be. And I really admire how well you manage to get everything done, and your superb leadership abilities," she said, hoping her use of flattery was not too little, not too much, but just right.

"I try my best," said Ms. Wicked, obviously pleased by the compliment. Then, she sent a hard look toward Malorette and Odette. "The guards tell me there has been some grumbling about the changes I've made, however. They tend to overhear such things." Alarm crossed the sisters' faces and the two of them wilted under the teacher's stern gaze.

Uh-oh, thought Goldie. If these girls got the idea that Ms. Wicked was starting to prefer her to them, they might get jealous and make trouble for her. Quickly, she said, "Really? Well, I can say for sure that Malorette and Odette have nothing but the highest praise for you. In fact, they see you as a role model! If it hadn't been for their encouragement," she said, glancing over at them with a look of false gratitude, "I would never have even dared think I might have a chance at joining your illustrious Society."

Ms. Wicked softened her gaze on the sisters. "Well, perhaps I was too hasty," she murmured. "My information may be faulty. Those guards aren't the brightest sometimes." Looking relieved, both girls picked up the sandwiches they'd put together and continued munching as they waited to see how the rest of the interview would unfold.

"Thing is," Goldie continued with false sincerity, "knowing how busy you are, I think it only fair that you should have students you can rely on — like Malorette, Odette, and me . . . and whoever else is already a member — to help out with the kind of tasks that you just don't have time for. And shouldn't be bothered with." She paused. "So . . . um . . . that's why I'd like to join. To . . . uh . . . make your life easier."

Ms. Wicked nodded. "Yes. That's a very good answer. Excellent, in fact."

Phew! thought Goldie.

"Let's move on from the interview to the next part of the application process, shall we?" Ms. Wicked suggested crisply. "What gift have you brought me?"

Gift? Goldie coughed, nearly choking on a piece of Black Forest ham. She couldn't believe Malorette and Odette had failed to mention that Ms. Wicked would expect a gift. She'd brought nothing except herself! She glared at the two sisters, but they only shrugged. *Thanks a lot!*

"I'm really sorry," Goldie fibbed. "I do have something for you, but I forgot it in my —"

"That's all right," interrupted Ms. Wicked. "I think I see something that will fit the bill nicely." She was staring at Goldie's hair. "Your pretty hairpin. Pearls go perfectly with my skin tone. May I?" Without waiting for an answer, she darted her hand forward. However, no sooner did she touch the pin than she gave a little jump and yelped in surprise. "Ow! That hairpin shocked me!" she exclaimed as she jerked her hand back.

Goldie's face went white. "Oh, I'm so sorry!" she gasped. "I can't imagine why that happened. Static electricity maybe?" she said. She pulled the hairpin from her golden locks and held it out to Ms. Wicked. "Please take it. I *want* you to have it. A gift." This was also a fib, since she really liked the hairpin and wanted to keep it. Besides being pretty, it was useful. Still, she did have other hairpins, though none as nice as this one, that she could use to unlock doors.

Ms. Wicked reached for it, then frowned and let her hand drop. "Never mind. I don't need scars on my hands from a wayward pin." Then, with a magnanimous sweep of her arm, she added, "We'll skip the gift part for now. We'll just go with the old saying that it's the thought that counts."

"Thanks!" Still wondering what in the world could have caused her hairpin to give off a shock, Goldie slipped the treacherous thing back into her hair and started to rise. "So if that's all . . ."

"It is not all. Sit, please," Ms. Wicked commanded. Leaning toward her again, she added, "You must know my stepdaughter, Snow, and her little friends. Yes?"

"Sure, I'm *acquainted* with them," Goldie replied carefully as she reseated herself. "They're in some of my classes, but I don't know them all that well."

Ms. Wicked nodded approvingly. "Keep it that way. I'm sorry to have to say this, since Snow is my own stepdaughter, but you'd do well to stay clear of her and her friends."

"Oh? Why?" Goldie asked, making her eyes innocently wide as she picked up one of Mistress Hagscorch's Heart-of-Despairberry Tarts. It moaned wretchedly, as all such tarts did when touched. She brought it up to her mouth and munched it. *Mmm.*

"Let's just say they don't share the same forward-looking goals that the Society and I have for the Academy," Ms. Wicked said diplomatically.

"Basically, they're troublemakers," Malorette growled darkly. She and Odette had been silent as ghosts up until now.

Goldie swallowed her mouthful of tart. "Wow, really? I didn't know," she said, acting dismayed. Of course, she didn't believe a bit of it.

Ms. Wicked flicked her hand as if waving away her concern. "Not to worry. There are many other students at the Academy much worthier of your friendship and time."

"Like us," smirked Odette, pointing to herself and Malorette.

Goldie flashed them a fake smile. "Right! And who else?" she asked, fishing for Society member names she could take back to share with Rapunzel and the other Grimm girls. "It would be helpful to know who to befriend and who not to."

Ms. Wicked cocked her head and smiled secretively. "All in good time," she said. Then she suddenly rose from her seat. "Thank you for coming, girls. I'll see you in class in a few minutes," she told Goldie, who had Scrying fourth period.

Goldie and Cinda's two stepsisters scrambled up from their chairs at the abrupt dismissal. In seconds, Ms. Wicked ushered them out of her office.

Ms. Jabberwocky wasn't around as the girls left. Goldie wondered if she was taking a jalapeño break outside somewhere on the Academy grounds. In spite of Principal R's famous temper tantrums, she'd kind of acted like she missed him and wished he were still in charge around here. Most GA students felt the same.

"So what happens next?" Goldie asked Malorette and Odette as they made their way back down the hall to the grand staircase.

Malorette shrugged. "Hard to say. You might not hear anything right away, though."

"And even if you *are* approved, you'll still need to pass a test," added Odette. "You'll be given a simple assignment —

some little job to prove your loyalty before you can officially become a member."

"What kind of job?" Goldie asked, frowning. First she'd heard of this!

"Like Principal W said, 'All in good time,'" Malorette replied mysteriously.

At the staircase, the girls separated to go to their classes. Minutes later, Goldie took her seat in Scrying class. During the entire period Ms. Wicked gave no sign that the two of them had talked at lunchtime. Which meant that Goldie left the room at the end of class no better informed as to how her interview had gone than before.

She climbed the stairs to the third floor for fifth period Calligraphy and Illuminated Manuscripts. It was a class she shared with both Red and Snow. She had just pushed through the door on the third-floor landing and started down the hall when a voice whispered in her ear, making her jump.

"Psst. It's me, Snow," said the voice. "Rapunzel and Red told Cinda and me what you're up to. Have you found out anything important yet? Society-wise, I mean?" Obviously, Snow was wearing her tiara and had made herself invisible so that no one would see them speaking.

"Nuh-uh," whispered Goldie, trying to keep her lips from moving too much as she walked along. "But I had an interview with Ms. Wicked, that is, your stepmom, during lunch. Still no idea if I'll get into E.V.I.L., though." She hesitated as a jackrabbit guard who was standing in the hallway swiveled one of its enormous ears her way and gave her the stink eye.

"Fingers crossed, then. See you in class," said Snow's voice. She might have been holding her crossed fingers up, but if she was, Goldie couldn't see them. Still, she nodded. At this, the guard's eyes narrowed.

"Yeah, I talk to myself a lot," she called to the jackrabbit with a laugh. "Guess it's only a problem if I start answering myself back, right?"

Looking unamused, the guard's nose twitched. "Move along. No loitering in the halls. Principal Wicked's orders!"

9

O-Key Doke

Back in her dorm room after dinner that evening, Goldie waited anxiously to hear if she'd been approved for membership in E.V.I.L. She tried working on a knitting project she needed to finish for Threads class by next Monday, but worries about her interview with Ms. Wicked wouldn't stop coming and she kept tangling her yarn and dropping stitches.

Polly knew about the interview, but Goldie hadn't yet filled her in on what happened during it. Unfortunately, they couldn't really discuss the matter openly, with spies like Malorette and Odette rooming right next door.

At last, feeling fidgety and desperate to know the answer to one burning question, Goldie grabbed a sheet of vellum paper from her desk drawer. Quickly, she wrote: *Ms. W's going to assign me a job to make me prove myself worthy of Society membership. What kind of job do you think it'll be?* Then she folded the note into a winged, birdlike shape and flew it up to Polly, who was already sitting on her bed in a nightgown, reading a book titled *Tea Parties of the Rich and Famous*.

When the paper bird landed on her book, Polly unfolded the note and read it. Then she scribbled an answer. After refolding the note, she flew it down to Goldie at her desk.

An evil one, she'd written as her reply.

Goldie grinned up at her, and they giggled. Then they both glanced warily at the wall next to Polly's bed and tried hard to stifle their laughter. It was always on their minds that Malorette and Odette might be listening through that very wall.

Goldie flattened the paper on her desk and wrote another message below the one Polly had written: *M and O said artifacts were going missing from the library a while back. Did they have anything to do with that? Wondering if they stole something to get into the Society. And if so, what?* Then she refolded the paper into a bird and flew it back up to Polly.

Polly read her note, then looked up and nodded in answer to her first question. Since there wasn't much room left on the paper bird to write anything, she silently mouthed the words *Peter Peter Pumpkineater's pumpkin* in answer to the second question. With her forefingers, she drew a big pumpkin in the air.

Goldie nodded to show that she understood. *Hmm,* she thought as she took out her pj's and started getting ready for bed. She'd seen Peter Peter's pumpkin on a shelf in the library not long ago, so that must mean it had been returned after Malorette and Odette stole it.

So maybe whatever evil thing she wound up doing as her Society initiation job could be undone afterward. She hoped so. Would she be asked to steal something as well? Luckily, locked doors and cabinets were nothing her pearl-flower hairpin couldn't handle.

"Wish you could've been at that meeting today," she said to Polly, forgetting to whisper as she climbed the ladder up to her bed.

"Shh!" hissed Polly, holding a finger to her lips.

Goldie froze halfway up the ladder. "Oops," she whispered before clambering the rest of the way up to snuggle under her covers.

"Scooch over," said Polly, making move-over motions and throwing her covers off. Goldie sat up and made space as she watched her scramble down her ladder and up Goldie's. Once they both were sitting on her bed, which was on the side of the room farthest from Malorette and Odette's room, they could talk more easily. Without having to worry about being overheard!

"So what all happened at your meeting, anyway?" Polly asked quietly.

"My hairpin zapped Ms. Wicked, for one thing," Goldie whispered back.

"Awesome!" Polly blurted, which made them both laugh again.

"Yeah, but last night in the dungeon, you, Red, and Rapunzel all held that pin with no problem. So I can't figure out why it zapped Ms. Wicked. It was rather *shocking*!" Goldie quipped. They cracked up at her little joke, having both caught a case of the giggles.

"It must have magic in it," Polly whispered back after they'd finally managed to get their giggles under control. Then she drew in a sharp breath. Turning to look at Goldie with excitement in her eyes, she said, "Hey! Do you think it could be your magic charm? They only work for the person they truly belong to, you know."

"Mm-hmm, I've heard that," Goldie replied, wrinkling her nose in thought. "The hairpin hasn't done any actual magic for me, though, unless you count zapping Ms. Wicked. And she wasn't trying to make it work for her when that happened. She was just trying to snatch it."

"But that could still be why it zapped her," said Polly. "Because charms avoid evil. They only come to those of good heart. Not a quality I'd use to describe Ms. You-Know-Who." She put on a hoity-toity face, nose in the air, one hand smoothing her hair as she tried to match Ms. Wicked's mannerisms.

Goldie joined in. "Students!" she whispered snootily. "Do my *badding*, I mean, my *bidding*. Or else! For I am the E.V.I.L.tastic principal of everything, not to mention a beauty queen, and don't you forget it." At this, both girls fell over on the bed, cracking up. It felt good to make fun of such a scary, powerful person as Ms. Wicked. Somehow, it made her and her possible plans for GA seem less terrifying, at least for the moment.

Eventually, their giggles turned to yawns, and Polly went back down the ladder at the end of Goldie's bed. After blowing out the candle that lit the girls' room, she climbed up to her own bed again. "Night-*TEA*-night," she called softly to Goldie.

"Night-*TEA*-night back with sugar on top," Goldie replied, smiling.

"And maybe a pinch of cinnamon," Polly added with a smile in her voice, too. Then she yawned.

Snuggling under her covers, Goldie thought about how cool it was that she and Polly had more to talk about now than just tea. If there was one *good* thing to be said about Ms. Wicked, it was that she had united students against her!

Goldie's eyes fluttered shut, but then they popped open again almost right away. Because something Polly had said about charms was still bugging her. "They only come to those of good heart," she'd said. Unfortunately, when Goldie thought about the role she played in the Goldilocks fairy tale, she wasn't actually sure she qualified for being of good heart. Even Ms. Wicked seemed to consider her the bad character in her tale.

She rolled over in bed and tried to focus on happier thoughts. If the pin really was her charm, what kind of magic might it be able to do? She pulled the covers up to her chin. Maybe it would grow into a sword like the needle charm of a daring princess named Briar Rose, who'd recently come to the Academy. Or expand and make itself into a cage or a ladder like Rapunzel's magical comb?

Red's cunning wicker basket could fetch things that fit inside it, but a hairpin had no storage space. And it seemed unlikely it could turn her invisible like Snow's tiara, either. She'd pressed on it plenty of times and nothing special had happened. It had proven itself to be a handy tool for picking locks. But just about any hairpin would work for that.

She squeezed her eyes shut and concentrated on the pin. She'd left it on her desk, and now she tried to make it come to her by magic. After a few minutes of nothing happening, she gave up. If the hairpin really was her special charm, she'd just have to wait for it to reveal what actual magic it could do.

After sixth period ended the next day, Goldie rounded a corner on the second floor and immediately spotted a group of students speaking to the gooseknob on the wall next to Ms. Queenharts's Comportment classroom. They'd discovered today's whereabouts of the library door.

Her breath caught. Was this a sign? A sign that she should search the library again? Would she find what she hadn't been able to last Monday — some clue that would lead her to Principal Rumpelstiltskin?

Wow, had that just been a few days ago? Seemed like ages had passed since she'd first spotted those growly bear guards, and Ms. Wicked had held her guard parade in the Great Hall. As she joined the line, Goldie realized she hadn't seen those bears since then. But maybe they were patrolling in the Gray Castle side of the Academy where she had no classes.

Afraid that the knob might recognize her from Monday night and cause a stink, Goldie kept her head down as she stood with the group. A nursery rhyme character named Jack Horner was in the middle of answering the goose head's riddle. Her timing was perfect. Once he had answered correctly, she was able to sneak through the door bunched in with the gaggle of taller students, totally undetected by that beaky knob. *Score!*

Flap! Flap! As she entered the library, a snow-white goose zoomed by overhead, zigzagging around the chandeliers hanging from the high ceiling. Then two more swooped in from the left and another from the right. Net bags dangled from the bright orange beak of each goose. One bag held books. The others held objects: red rubber balls the size of large tomatoes, a huge jar of brightly colored gumballs, and cloth dolls with button eyes and yarn for hair.

The geese paid no attention to her or to any of the other students in the library as she made a beeline for Section *G*. Only this time, she wasn't heading for the shelves of Grimm fairy tales. She was heading for the Grimm brothers' room. Though Goldie had never been inside it herself, everyone in Grimmlandia knew it was the most magical place in the library. And since she hadn't been able to find Principal R's tale on the main library shelves last Monday, she wondered if maybe Ms. Goose had stuck it in the Grimm brothers' room for added security.

When she finally arrived outside the room she sought, its door was standing open a few inches. She paused to study its locking mechanism. To a lock-picking girl like her, such things were a matter of professional interest! As she examined the door's lock more closely, she saw it had three keyholes. "You sure are well fortified," she exclaimed softly.

She was stalling, of course. Because actually stepping inside this room was going to be a rather daunting test for her. Rumor had it that there was a protective force field around this room, which somehow repelled evil. No Society members — not even Ms. Wicked — could pass over this threshold and enter. So if this most magical room allowed Goldie inside, it would have to mean she wasn't truly evil herself!

She pushed the door wide and peered into the room. It was lined with bookshelves and stuffed with items and furnishings that had no doubt once belonged to the Grimm brothers. Dozens of portraits hung on one wall, including seven in carved golden frames that were grouped together in the center. She recognized the portraits of Jacob and Wilhelm Grimm among them.

For a moment, she braced herself. "Here goes nothing," she whispered. Then, in a burst of energy, she sprang over the threshold and zipped to the center of the room. She stood there, her shoulders hunched, her whole body tight.

Nothing happened. The room *hadn't* rejected her!

"Hooray! I'm not evil!" Goldie cried. Then she did a little twirly happy dance right where she stood. She was about to go look more closely at the portraits when a glass paper-weight in the shape of a goldfish suddenly lifted off an ornate desk across the room and came flying at her.

"Yikes!" She ducked, fearing the room had decided to attack her after all. But the paperweight merely circled around her and sailed off to land atop the head of a statue at the back of the room.

"Phew! That was close." As she straightened again, other objects began to move around her under their own power. A deck of cards shuffled itself in midair and then the cards started to flip themselves over one at a time onto a small antique side table, in what looked like a game of soli-taire. *Weird.*

She whipped around when the crank on a jack-in-the-box in a corner of the room began to turn, playing "Pop Goes the Weasel." At the end of the tune, a bouncy clown with a wide red smile sprang up from the box, spreading its arms wide. Then it popped back down inside the box, and the crank began to turn again.

"Well, you are a fantastical room for sure," Goldie mur-mured as she gazed around it. "What secrets do you hold that could need such strong protection anyway? Clues to our real principal's whereabouts perhaps?" These were questions worth asking because you never knew — the room might've answered. After all, a talking room would have fit right in at Grimm Academy! Unfortunately, this room didn't answer back.

Going over to the bookshelves, she started looking for the Rumpelstiltskin tale. But though she searched high and low, pulling each book out in turn, she didn't find it. She did find something else of interest, though. A thin booklet titled *All About Magic Charms*.

Taking it over to the ornate desk, she sat in the large tufted leather chair before it and crisscrossed her legs in the comfy seat. Doing her best to ignore the objects whizzing by overhead and the toy train that had begun to chug along a track that ran around the room, she began to read.

Most of the stuff in the booklet she already knew. Such as that magic charms came only to those of good heart. And that if you were lucky enough to get a charm, its magic powers would reveal themselves gradually. Also, that a magic charm would work only for the person it belonged to. On the last page, she came across a fact she hadn't known:

Once you find your magic charm — or it finds you — your bond with it can never be broken. In times of trouble, whether you and your charm are together or apart, it can always send you to a place of safety.

"Hear that?" she exclaimed aloud, reaching up to pat her pearl-flower hairpin. "If you are my magic charm, it means you have the power to rescue me if I'm ever in trouble. Which would make you one grimmazing hairpin."

Glancing at the wall over the desk, she caught sight of the Grimm coat of arms that hung there. It looked like a big shield with various gold emblems on it. She shuddered and pushed back in her chair, remembering rumors that students had occasionally seen an eyeball or a nose poking out of the shield. Luckily, nothing of that sort happened now.

Having finished the booklet, she went over and slid it back onto the shelf where she'd found it. After one last disappointed scan of the room, she turned to leave. She had taken only a single step out of the door and into the main library when a crystal marble came rolling straight toward her across the library floor. It bumped into the toe of her slipper and stopped. She bent to pick it up.

"A message marble!" she exclaimed aloud. Such marbles contained information from their senders that was of immediate importance. This one had the sender's initials — *P.W.* — carved on it. *Who?* Wait! It must be from (acting) Principal Wicked! Her heart started beating faster. She had a feeling she was about to be given orders that could make or break her chances of getting accepted into the E.V.I.L. Society.

Goldie gazed down at the clear marble lying in her palm and waited for its message to appear. Within seconds, the marble changed form, expanding into a ball of pale gray mist that filled her hand. A message ran across the orb of mist in a continuous line. Quickly, she read the words before they could disappear forever:

Dear Society Candidate: Your job, should you decide to accept it, is to open the safe located in the library office and bring me what's inside. I've arranged for Ms. Goose to be away at an Academy staff meeting now, so attempt this assignment immediately! Ask no questions. Simply follow my orders. Afterward, keep this message marble with you at all times.

When Goldie finished reading, the mist contracted into a solid crystal marble again, and the initials *P.W.* disappeared from it. She stared at it in dismay, murmuring, "A safe? Ms. Wicked wants me to break into a *safe*?"

Had Ms. Wicked somehow found out about her lock-picking skills? Why else would she ask her to do this, since everyone knew safes were usually locked? Maybe that kangaroo guard had guessed about the lock? Anyway, this was definitely also a test of her ability and willingness to carry out orders. And the last part of the message — about keeping the marble with her — made her think Ms. Wicked must be planning to use it to communicate with her whenever she felt the need.

More than a little wary, Goldie slipped the marble into her pocket and got moving. She'd never been in the librarian's office before, but she knew where it was. Back near the main library entrance, across from that tall checkout desk she'd hidden behind on Monday night.

After quickly making her way there, she waited outside the door marked OFFICE until no one was nearby and no geese were flying overhead. Then she slipped inside the unlocked room, shut the door, and took three steps inside. *Crunch, crunch, crunch.* She looked down in surprise to see that the entire office floor was covered with crisp, clean, sweet-smelling hay! Probably it was there for the comfort of the geese that worked in the library.

She scanned the room and started rummaging around, looking for a safe. Brightly painted red, yellow, and blue file cabinets stood against the wall to her left. Beyond them stretched a long countertop that was piled with stacks of old books. From the supplies nearby — needles and thread, tape and glue — she guessed these books were awaiting repairs.

The cupboards above the counter were decorated with nursery rhyme scenes. Among them were the three little kittens wearing mittens, and the cow jumping over the moon. She opened the cupboards to see if the safe was inside one of them but found only alphabet blocks with more nursery rhyme scenes and letters on them.

If she had to use one word to describe the room, she'd call it cozy. It felt like a nest. It made her wonder if Ms. Goose had the power to shape-shift into a real goose when she wanted to. The thought made her smile.

Just then, a movement to her right caught her eye. Was it Ms. Goose coming back? Her breath caught in her throat as she whipped around. How was she going to explain being in here?

Phew! "A mobile, that's all," she murmured. One with a bunch of carved white porcelain geese dangling and spinning around in the air. Nothing to get alarmed about after all.

"Quit being so jumpy," she scolded herself. But she couldn't help it. Was she really going to steal something and deliver it into the no-good rotten hands of E.V.I.L.? She wished she had more time to think. But Ms. Wicked had purposely rushed her, giving her no time to consider the right or wrong of carrying out her demand. Obviously, she just expected members of the Society to obey her orders, no questions asked.

Since she saw nothing that looked like a safe anywhere, Goldie went over to sit on a mound of hay in the center of the room to better study her surroundings. *Crunch! Crunch! Crunch!*

She had expected the mound to be somewhat soft, but found it so hard and round that she immediately slid off. *Huh?* Turning, she brushed away some hay from the mound and soon uncovered a large gray object. It was about the size of a big beach ball. Only, it was shaped more like a gigantic goose egg! She poked it. It was metal, not egg-shell. She poked it again. *Creak!* Oh, no! She'd accidentally dislodged it from its perch! It rolled crazily across the floor stopping only when it bumped into Ms. Goose's desk. *Thunk!*

Goldie ran over to the metal egg-thing. Planting both her hands against it, she started pushing, rolling it back toward the mound. Halfway there, she stopped. Because she'd noticed something. There was a little door on the side of the metal egg! With a keyhole! Could this egg-thing be the safe she sought?

Kneeling beside it, she slid her trusty pearl-flower hair-pin into its lock. After gently fiddling around a bit, she felt it give. *Snap!* She stared eagerly as the door sprang open. To her surprise, inside that egg was another egg with another door. Also locked. She poked at it with her hairpin. Eventually, that lock sprang open, too, to reveal yet another egg with another locked door.

She did this six times before she finally opened the last door in the last egg, way in the middle of the biggest egg.

The space inside the last, smallest egg safe was only just big enough for her to fit her hand inside. And when she did, her fingers connected with a large ring with some keys dangling from it. *Why keep keys in a safe?* she wondered as she drew out the ring.

"No matter. I did it! I accomplished the mission Ms. Wicked gave me, so that should make her happy," she said to herself. She slammed the egg doors shut one by one, then rolled the egg back atop its mound. Slipping the keys into her pocket alongside the message marble, she started out of Ms. Goose's office. But as her hand touched the doorknob, a question stopped her.

Why had Ms. Wicked needed *her* to fetch this key ring? Surely, she could have gotten into this safe herself if she really wanted to. As acting principal, she must have access to all kinds of keys — including skeleton ones, obviously — that opened things around the school.

Was there a protection spell on Ms. Goose's office like the one on the Grimm brothers' room that kept evil people like Ms. Wicked out? *Hmm. The Grimm brothers' room.* Suddenly, Goldie remembered the unusual lock with three keyholes on the Grimm brothers' room door. Taking the ring of keys from her pocket, she took time to actually count its keys. There were three. The same number of keyholes on that door.

Carefully, she studied the notches at the ends of each key. She had an excellent memory for the shapes of keys and locks. And there was no doubt in her mind that these three keys would fit each of the three keyholes in the lock on the Grimm brothers' room door!

She pursed her lips. What if sticking these keys in those keyholes could somehow break the protective spell on the Grimm brothers' room and allow evil to cross its threshold? Keeping evil from entering that room must be important, or the room wouldn't need protection and Ms. Goose wouldn't have locked away these keys.

She stared at them, shaking her head. No way could she give these keys to E.V.I.L. That would be a truly evil act that might be disastrous for the entire realm of Grimmlandia, for all she knew.

Retracing her steps, she stooped beside the egg safe. One by one, she reopened its doors. After replacing the ring of keys inside the smallest egg, she relocked the doors again. Then she slipped out of the office unnoticed and made her way out of the library.

"Great, just great. So now what are you going to tell Ms. Wicked in Scrying class tomorrow?" she muttered to herself as she made her way to the Great Hall for dinner. She practiced a possible fib she might use: "Ms., I mean, Principal Wicked?" she said in a higher-than-normal voice.

"Turns out there were too many students around to get into Ms. Goose's office yesterday and I was scared I'd get caught."

No. That might make Ms. Wicked think she was too chicken to be a member of E.V.I.L. So maybe she should say instead: "Principal Wicked, I'm so sorry, but when I unlocked Ms. Goose's egg safe, it was totally empty."

She nodded to herself as she turned a corner. "Yeah, that's better. Then at least she won't be able to blame me for not even trying to complete her little job."

Hearing her mutterings, a badger on patrol in the hallway shot her a suspicious look. Sending him a nervous smile, she stopped talking to herself and hurried the rest of the way to the Great Hall.

10

Heart Island

When Goldie awoke the next morning, Foulsmell was on her mind and in her nose. No, not the prince. A real actual foul smell was in the air and had wafted to her nose, confusing her brain for a few seconds. Something was burning.

"Think Principal Rumpelstiltskin is back?" she asked, brightening at the thought that he might be over in his office doing alchemy. When there was no answer, she sat up and looked across at Polly's bed. It was empty. She must've gotten up early and left for breakfast in the Hall already. Quickly, Goldie scampered down her bed ladder and got dressed.

On her way into the Great Hall, she happened to pass the actual Prince Foulsmell. She was pretty sure he saw her, but he pretended not to. Which made her feel kind of rotten. As rotten as the faint burning smell lingering around the kitchen today. Mistress Hag*scorch* must've *scorch*ed something, she decided even before she spotted the handwritten sign in the breakfast line. It read:

Please pardon the smell due to accidental guard-tail scorching this morning.

Could happen again. Guards (especially badgers) beware and keep out!

Goldie couldn't help grinning over that. From the sign's wording she gathered the guards had been in the kitchen and Mistress Hagscorch was fed up with the intrusion. Once Goldie was through the line, she stopped herself from joining her newest friends. Ms. Wicked had warned her to stay away from her stepdaughter, Snow, and Snow's companions. However, she hadn't said anything about other "good" fairy-tale characters. Did she expect her to hang out only with evil ones?

She looked over at Malorette and Odette. They'd been nice to her since Wednesday's interview, but so far they hadn't asked her on other outings or asked her to sit with them, either. Were they waiting for Ms. Wicked's decision before wasting any more time on her? Typical. Their friendship offer was apparently *conditional*.

She hoped that wasn't true for Snow, and the other Grimm girls, too. If Goldie didn't make the E.V.I.L. Society, she wouldn't be able to bring Snow and her friends the information they sought. Would they drop her since she'd therefore be of no use to them? Would their offer of friendship prove conditional in the end as well? Her throat tightened up just thinking about it.

Since she wasn't sure of Ms. Wicked's rules regarding who could hang out with whom, she decided to sit alone. *Borrring!* She glanced down the table at Foulsmell. Not wanting to jeopardize her chances of getting into the Society, she'd been cautious about saying anything to him in Bespellings class yesterday. After all, he was a friend of Rapunzel's, who was also a friend of Snow's. He'd looked kind of hurt and annoyed about it, though. Just like he was acting toward her now.

Who could blame him? She had to find a way to apologize for Malorette and Odette's horridness to him two days ago and explain why she couldn't really talk to him, at least for a while. She didn't dare tell him about trying to get into the Society, but she needed him to understand that *she* didn't think of him as a puppy dog!

So as she was leaving Bespellings class later that morning, she sneaked him a note. It read:

Hi, Foulsmell.

I'm worried I hurt your feelings when Malorette and Odette were mean to you in the hall. You and I are friends (I hope!), and I should have stood up for you. I'm sorry. Unfortunately, it would not be a good idea for us to be seen hanging out right now. Ask Rapunzel and she'll tell you why.

Talk soon, when it's safe,

Goldie

Foulsmell looked surprised and puzzled as she pressed the note into his hand, but then he gave her a quick nod, as though he understood her need for secrecy. It was possible that Rapunzel had already told him what was going on.

She waited till the very end of fourth-period Scrying before summoning the courage to go up to Ms. Wicked's desk to tell her the lie she'd decided on last night.

"Um, so I opened Ms. Goose's egg safe," she began.

Ms. Wicked leaned forward eagerly. "Yes? And?"

"I'm sorry, but it was empty."

"Empty!" Goldie strove to keep a neutral look on her face as Ms. Wicked studied her expression carefully. In the end, the teacher seemed to believe her. "The wily old goose must've taken out those k — I mean whatever was in the safe before the meeting." She heaved a deep, disgruntled sigh. "Never mind. I'll come up with a different test for you. It'll have to wait till tomorrow, though. I've called a meeting of the guards for this afternoon."

"Then I'm still in the running for the Society?" Goldie asked.

Ms. Wicked nodded regally.

"Gosh! Thanks!" Goldie forced a bright smile, then turned to go.

A hand grabbed her arm, stopping her. A hand with long, glossy red fingernails.

"W-what?" asked Goldie.

"Do you still have the message marble I sent you?" the teacher asked.

Goldie nodded.

"Good," said Ms. Wicked. She let go of her arm. "Take your seat." There was a self-satisfied glint in her eye as she dismissed her. *What was that about?* wondered Goldie.

Being in limbo this way — unable to hang out with friends and waiting to find out what her evil assignment would be — was not fun at all. So when Goldie went up to her room after Friday's classes and found a small bouquet of flowers on her desk, she felt both excited and nervous. Were they from Ms. Wicked?

"What's this?" she asked Polly, who had only just stopped by to put on boots. Apparently, she and her nursery rhyme pals, Jack and Jill and Mary Mary Quite Contrary, were going to hike up some hill and then purposely take a spill, rolling back down it for kicks. Goldie was so desperate for fun, she'd halfway considered going with them when

Polly had explained the plan just now. But she wasn't sure what Ms. Wicked would think of her hanging out with nursery rhyme characters. Besides, she hadn't actually been invited.

"The flowers? They flew in the window by bluebird delivery from the Bouquet Garden a few minutes ago," Polly said as she finished lacing up her boots. "I figured they must be for you since no one ever sends me flowers." She grinned over at Goldie. "Tea, yes. Flowers, no."

Goldie bent over her desk to sniff the bouquet, which was made up of yellow roses, white daisies, orange lilies, and yellow sunflowers. "Mmm, nice."

An extraordinary variety of flowers grew in Grimm Academy's Bouquet Garden. Unlike most flowers, however, the ones in the GA garden actually bloomed together in attractive combinations all on one bush. So with a single flick of your wrist, you could pick a beautifully arranged ready-made bouquet of many kinds of flowers.

"Well, I'm off!" said Polly, heading for the curtain door at the entrance to their room. "See you!"

"Later," Goldie called after her, without looking around. Glimpsing a small card hidden among the flowers, she pulled it out. *For Goldie*, it said on one side. She flipped over the card and read what was scribbled on the back:

Thanks for your note.

Need to talk.

Four thirty.

Heart Island.

– F.

These flowers were from Foulsmell? She couldn't have been more surprised if someone had hit her in the face with them. She'd never gotten flowers from a boy before. Or from anyone! Her aunt had allergies and disapproved of flowers, especially cut ones. "Frivolous and unnecessarily showy," she would have likely proclaimed this bouquet to be. But Goldie thought it was beautiful.

She reread Foulsmell's note. She guessed the flowers must mean he'd accepted the apology in her note to him. But he had ignored the bit about them not hanging out. Why did they *need* to meet on Heart Island?

Come to think of it, though, she'd been kind of wanting to check the island for those three bear guards. She'd asked around and it seemed that no one else had seen them since they'd marched into the Great Hall last Monday either. What could they be up to? And were they up to it on Heart Island? If so, sneaking around there was a must!

Just then the Hickory Dickory Dock clock bonged in the

Hall, the sound echoing throughout the school. It was almost four. She could row to the island by four thirty if she left now. So . . .

Her feet decided what to do before her mind did. They carried her across the room, where she grabbed a hooded blue cloak from her closet. She was going to the island!

After making sure the message marble was still in the pocket of her gown (in case Ms. Wicked sent her a message with a new assignment), she was out the tower door, down the stairs, and across the drawbridge. She wasn't surprised she didn't meet any guards since Ms. Wicked had said she'd called them together for a meeting that afternoon. Perfect. Goldie only hoped that the bear guards would be at the meeting, too.

At the dock, Goldie untethered a single-bench swan boat and was quickly on her way. She had paddled only a few lengths downriver, however, when a breeze whipped back her hood. Quickly, she slipped it over her hair again and darted a look across the river at the Academy. From the corner of her eye, she thought she saw a couple of figures in a tower window. Had someone seen her? If so, her bright, golden locks would be a dead giveaway as to who she was.

She squinted at the window, but now it looked empty. Not that it really mattered one way or the other. It was perfectly fine for her to be out boating on the river. She just didn't like the idea of being spied on.

On the dot of four thirty, she pulled up to the dock on Heart Island and found Foulsmell waiting for her, a bag slung over one of his shoulders. As she leaped out, he tied up her boat next to the one he must have come in.

"Hurry," he said, taking her arm. "There could be spies."

She might've thought him overly concerned if she hadn't been worrying about the same thing just minutes ago.

"Thanks for the flowers," she told him as they rushed for cover. Anyone approaching the island would see their boats, but they wouldn't know who had arrived in them. Once they reached a thick grove of alder trees, they slowed, continuing on toward the island's center.

"You got the bouquet? Oh, yeah, of course you did. Duh. You wouldn't have gotten the note and come here otherwise," said Foulsmell. He seemed a little nervous and shy. Should she apologize more for the whole puppy thing? Or maybe he just wanted to forget about it. She sure did!

When Foulsmell bent to set down his bag, Goldie sat on a stump and looked around. Heart Island was pretty flat, a lot like Maze Island. Which made it the perfect place to hold events and festivals like the one students had organized to earn money for the Academy not long ago. The very one where Ms. Wicked had picked the animal blossom guards from all those tongue twister plants. There was plenty of space here to put up booths, games, makeshift stages, and even large tents for dances. Still, there were lots of trees, too. Trees that could hide a house for bear guards.

"Hello?" said Foulsmell, leaning over so his face was in her line of sight.

"Oh, sorry, did you say something?" she asked him.

"Mm-hmm. I said Rapunzel told me what you were up to. Trying to join E.V.I.L." He frowned at her. "Sounds pretty dangerous."

Goldie felt a sharp tug of annoyance. Her aunt had often looked at her like Foulsmell was doing now, especially when she was unhappy about whatever Goldie was up to. She stood and folded her arms, glaring at him.

"It's nice of you to be so concerned," she said in a tight, overly sweet voice that implied the opposite. "But this is my business and it's something I really feel I have to do."

"I was afraid you'd say that," Foulsmell replied with a sigh. "So I brought these."

Stooping and reaching into his bag, he produced two magic wands. Seeing her immediate interest, he handed her one. "Like 'em?" he asked, wiggling his eyebrows mischievously. "I 'borrowed' them from Ms. Blue's room. Figured you should at least have some kind of protection if you're going to keep on with this crazy scheme." He sounded rather pleased with himself.

"Good idea, only we never quite mastered the whole wand and bubble thing, so . . ." Goldie began.

"Exactly. So I thought we should practice. Which is why I suggested we come out here. Knowing more than one class's worth of bubble-using spells would have been cool, but since somebody magicked the chapter on Defensive Magic right out of our Handbooks, we'll have to —"

"You noticed that, too?" interrupted Goldie.

He shrugged and turned to lead her toward a clearing. "Hard not to."

"Ms. Wicked's handiwork, do you think?" she asked, skipping to catch up to him.

"Most likely. E.V.I.L. must not consider defensive magic to be important 'for everyone's safety,' as she's always putting it."

"Or maybe they figure it's important for *E.V.I.L.'s* safety that we *don't* learn defensive magic," Goldie mused. Quickly, she told him about the meeting of the guards Ms. Wicked had called that very afternoon, and they speculated on what it might be about.

Foulsmell stopped in the clearing and ran his fingers through his tangled brown hair. "Remember back in class how I said I like to give everyone the benefit of the doubt?"

"Uh-huh." Her cheeks went warm as she remembered that she'd called him *Fool*smell for saying it. "You said that being suspicious of others all the time isn't a very fun way to live."

He looked pleased that she remembered what he'd said. "It's not, usually. But, well, I've decided you were probably right to suspect Ms. Wicked after all. Too bad for her and her evil empire, though. Because we've got these!" He held up his wand, swishing it in a zigzag of expert moves. "Ready for a little bubblizing?"

"Definitely." Thrusting off her hooded cloak, Goldie tossed it over a large flat rock nearby, then grinned at him. "Here goes nothing." She spun her wand around in a series of quick circles, and so did he.

His first bubble was a half-inflated flop, but he only laughed and quickly popped it. His second surrounded him completely, and was round and strong. He bounced around in it carefully, testing its strength.

Goldie's first bubble had been a complete one that was only a little misshapen, so she too tried some bouncing. When she managed a bounce as high as a nearby tree branch, she stretched out both arms from within the bubble to grasp it. Catching hold, she hung from the branch, pleased when her bubble didn't pop.

"Nice!" Foulsmell encouraged, while bouncing in a circle around the clearing. When he drew closer, he said, "By the way, Rapunzel said to tell you she and Snow and their friends discovered that some of the animal guards are snitching on students . . . teachers, too . . . and reporting back to Ms. Wicked whatever they see or hear."

"I know." It was what Ms. Wicked had implied at lunch on Wednesday, and Goldie had already guessed that the kangaroo guard probably had ratted on her about picking the dungeon lock. "What I *don't* know is what Ms. Wicked would think about me having any non-evil friends," she went on as she dangled from the tree. "So like I said in my note, we probably shouldn't *hang* out." With that, she released her grip on the branch she'd been hanging from.

When she hit the ground, her bubble bounced her right back up again. Then down. Then up again. She tried moving around the clearing. *Boing! Boing!*

"Hey, this is fun!" But then she got a little too boldly enthusiastic. When she landed at an angle, she suddenly found herself rolling down a hill.

"Whoa!" she shouted as she hurtled toward the bottom. So this was Polly, Jack and Jill, and Mary Mary's idea of fun? Scrambling your brains by rolling down hills? Nuh-uh! Eventually, she managed to direct her bubble so it bounced

off a tree trunk, then off another and another, finally slow-
ing herself.

Foulsmell bounced up to her. "You okay?" he asked
breathlessly.

"Yeah. You?" she asked, breathless, too.

He nodded.

"Enough! I need a bubble break." *Pop!* Goldie poked her
bubble from the inside with the sharp tip of her wand.

"Okay, I'm beat, too," he said, popping his bubble as
well. "That was a workout!"

"Yeah, fun, though," she said. They sat in the grass at
the bottom of the hill, waiting for their hearts to slow, then
finally got up and walked back toward the dock.

"I don't think anyone spotted us here," Foulsmell noted,
looking around.

"Yeah. And I wore my hooded cloak on the way over to
cover my —" Suddenly, she broke off. "Oh! Hey, I forgot my
cloak back on the rock near our practice area."

"I'll go back and get it for you," Foulsmell volunteered.

Quickly, Goldie shook her head. They were just steps
away from the dock by now. She could see their two boats
still tied up to it. "No. You go on ahead," she suggested.
"That way if Ms. Wicked's meeting is over and there are any
snoopy guards around, they won't see us arrive at the
Academy together."

"You sure?" he asked. He seemed reluctant to leave her alone, as if he thought it too dangerous.

"Mm-hmm," she said firmly. Waving her wand, she added with a grin, "If I get in trouble, I'll make a bubble!"

He laughed.

"Go ahead. I've got this wand for protection. I'll be fine, I promise," she told him.

"Okay. See you soon. But I'll pretend I don't see you, so no one will know we're friends."

"Sounds like a plan," she replied, grinning at what he'd said. *Friends.* It appeared their friendship had been rescued from certain doom after all! How grimmtastic was that?

As Foulsmell climbed into his boat, Goldie went back for her cloak. It was actually a lucky thing she'd left it behind, because even though she hadn't done it on purpose, it gave her an excuse to remain on the island a little while on her own. She was pretty sure Foulsmell wouldn't have approved of what she was about to do now. And though she could've used his help, this was something she wanted to do on her own.

Earlier, in mid bubble bounce, she'd noticed a grove in the distance that was not too small. With trees not too short. Yes, that grove had looked to be *just right* for a bear guard hideout! And now was her chance to search for it.

After putting on her cloak and tucking her practice wand deep inside its pocket, she started toward the grove of trees at the far side of the island. When she neared it, she climbed a tree to have a look around. And there, in a small clearing at the very center of the grove, just as she'd somehow known it would be, she spied a cute little cottage. One with a bear paw–shaped welcome mat outside the front door. *Score!*

She climbed down, remembering the squeaky voice of the smallest bear that night in the library: *"Don't forget, Principal W told us a special visitor will be waiting for us there!"* In the cottage they called home, he'd meant. This cottage, she bet.

Was their "special visitor" still inside? A visitor called Principal R, who was really more like a prisoner? She'd better go have a look!

11

The Cottage

Low-hanging branches snatched at Goldie's cloak and hair as she threaded her way through the grove's thick trees to the clearing at its center. Finally, she drew near enough to study the cottage from the protection of bushes surrounding it.

Were the three bears at Ms. Wicked's meeting with all the other guards? Or were they here, inside? She tiptoed and kept a careful lookout as she approached, just in case.

The cottage was plain, with wooden sides painted white. There was a window beside the door, but its dark green shutters were closed. No matter what Malorette and Odette thought, Goldie wasn't the type to break into houses, so she tapped at the door.

"Hello?" she called. No one answered. She rattled the knob, but as she expected, the door was locked. "Are you in there, Principal R?" she called out, louder than before.

Still no answer. But if the principal *was* here being kept prisoner, he might be bound and gagged and wouldn't be able to answer. Or he could be asleep, or under a spell, or . . . well . . . any number of things, really. There was no way around it. She had to get inside. Her mind made up, she slid her gleaming pearl-flower hairpin from her golden hair and picked the front door lock.

Once over the doorstep, she called Principal R's name again. Still no answer. "Rumpelstiltskin?" she tried. If he was inside, hearing her call out his full name would be bound to send him into a tantrum, right? And that would create enough noise that she'd certainly hear him. But the only sound she heard was the *drip*, *drip*, *drip* of the kitchen faucet.

She moved farther into the cottage, holding her breath. It seemed to have only one room, which was sparsely furnished with just a round table and three chairs, all of different sizes. No Principal R hidden here. How disappointing!

Still, the bears might've left some helpful clues about his whereabouts if they knew where he was or if he *had* been here. They seemed to have taken off for their meeting at GA in a hurry, she noticed as she crept around the kitchen. They hadn't eaten their supper. There were still three bowls on the table, each full of porridge. *Mmm. Porridge.*

It was her dinnertime by now, and she was hungry. And this porridge smelled delicious. But she was determined not to eat the guards' food, since that reminded her too much of her tale.

"Besides," she muttered aloud, "I am not a thief!" So no way would she eat that porridge. Absolutely not. Nuh-uh. Still, she was so very hungry. She sniffed at the porridge in one of the bowls and her stomach growled. "Mmm. Cinnamon," she murmured. Just how she liked it.

The bears would probably only throw out the porridge when they returned home, so would it really hurt anything if she ate some of it? No, of course not.

"It would actually be wasteful just to leave it," Goldie said to herself. "I'll only have a little." She found a clean spoon and dipped it into the biggest bowl. But when she tried the porridge in the big bowl, she nearly burned her tongue. "Yikes!" she said, fanning her mouth. "Too hot!"

She tried the porridge in the medium-size bowl next. "Yuck. Too cold," she murmured. Which was odd when she thought about it, since you'd expect the porridge in both bowls to be nearly the same temperature. But whatever!

Luckily, the porridge in the smallest bowl was neither too hot nor too cold, but just the right temperature. And with exactly the right amount of brown-sugar sweetness, too. "Yum," she sighed. And before she knew it, she'd eaten it all up.

"Oh, no," she said, staring into the empty bowl in dismay. "I can't believe I did that! Well, surely Ms. Wicked will serve food to the guards at their meeting like she did at my E.V.I.L. interview, so they won't go hungry."

Still, to make up for what she'd done, or maybe in hopes the bears might forget they'd left porridge waiting, she decided to wash the dishes. First, she gathered up the bowls and spoons and carried them over to the counter. She had to stand on tiptoe to lift them over her head and set them down in the sink. Short as she was and as tall as bears were, she couldn't quite reach well enough to wash them.

"No problem," she said to herself. "I'll just drag over a chair to stand on." The largest chair in the room proved too heavy for her to budge even an inch from its place at the table. And she could see at a glance that the generously cushioned medium-size chair would be too soft and lumpy for standing on. But the smallest chair — a simple straight-backed wooden chair with a woven seat — seemed like it would work just right.

She dragged it to the sink and climbed up to stand on it. She'd only just filled up the sink with hot water and soap and begun to scrub the dishes, however, when . . . *rrrip!* Her feet crashed through the woven seat!

How grimmawful! she thought as she freed herself from the chair. *Nothing about this search is going at all well.*

No sooner had she pulled herself out of the chair than she heard a scratching noise. It seemed to be coming from behind a door at the back of the cottage. She'd thought at first that the door must lead outside, but it flashed on her now that it probably opened into a bedroom since the bears would surely need a place to sleep.

"Ha! Maybe Principal R is here after all!" Goldie whispered to herself. Leaving the dishes in the sink, she dashed over to investigate. When she opened the door, which did indeed lead to a bedroom, a mouse scampered past her. Being unafraid of mice, she did *not* scream. She did feel like sighing, however. Because she could see at a glance that Principal R was nowhere around. It was only the mouse she'd heard.

Hey! Could he be under one of the beds? There were three of them. But before she could check, she noticed something on the bedside table. A book! Not just any book, though. One of the Grimm fairy tale books from the GA library. The very one she'd been looking for all this time. The one containing Principal R's tale! What was it doing here? Was it only a coincidence that the bears had it?

Taking the book with her, she lay on her stomach upon the biggest bed and opened the book to read. Unfortunately, the bed's wide, stiff mattress was so uncomfortable it made her squirm. So she picked up the book and moved to the medium-size bed. Its mattress was as soft and lumpy as the medium-size chair in the other room. Which was no good for reading, either. The smallest bed, however, was not too hard, not too soft, but just right.

She kicked off her shoes and turned to the beginning of Principal R's tale. Would this book yield clues as to where he could be? She hoped so. She was determined to find him. Because how else was she going to become the hero of the school?

However, before she could finish even a single paragraph, she heard voices outside the cottage. *Oh, no!* It sounded like the three bears had returned!

"Well, he*rrr*e we are, home again," growled a low voice she recognized as the biggest of the three bears, code name Papa Bear.

As she leaped from the small bed, she heard an impatient voice say, "Well, hurry up. Who's got the keys?" That was Ms. Wicked! What was *she* doing here?

"Just a sec. I hid them under the doormat," said the squeaky voice of Baby Bear.

"You did what? What kind of security guards are you? That's the first place a burglar would look, you know," said

Ms. Wicked. Which started an argument among the bears about who should be in charge of the keys from then on.

Meanwhile, Goldie set the book back where she'd found it and looked around wildly for a way to escape. But the bedroom had no outside door. No window, either. Its only source of light shone through the door that opened to the main room of the cottage. Quickly, she shut it almost all the way, leaving a small gap so she could still hear what was going on out there. Then she dropped to the floor, grabbed her shoes, and rolled under the small bed to hide. As she lay there on her back, trying to get comfortable, her arm brushed against something crumpled and soft.

She reached for it and held it before her face, trying to focus. A hat? A tall one that looked exactly like the one Principal R wore! Did this mean he *had* been here at some point but then escaped? Or maybe the guards had moved him somewhere else? Either way, maybe he'd left this hat behind on purpose, as a clue to show that he'd been here. A thrill swept over her. She'd found a clue to the mystery of his disappearance! Quickly, she folded the hat as small as she could and rammed it into the pocket of her cloak.

Just then, she heard the key clink in the outside lock. "What? We didn't even need the key," the Baby Bear guard squeaked in surprise. "The door was already open!"

"Are you sure you didn't just forget to lock it?" growled the voice of the medium-size bear. Code name Mama Bear, Goldie recalled.

"Sure, I'm sure. I'm always careful to check," Baby Bear replied.

Goldie's heart leaped into her throat as footsteps sounded inside the cottage. Immediately, Papa Bear let out a roar. "We left bowls of po*rrr*idge sitting on the table," he growled. "Someone's stolen them!"

"And my chair!" howled Baby Bear. "Someone broke it!"

"I think I can guess who," said Ms. Wicked. "Didn't you wonder who brought over the swan boat we saw at the dock? One of the Academy students. Luckily, I've been tracking her movements, something you imbeciles should have thought of." Her high heels clicked as she moved around in the cottage's main room.

Goldie gulped. Had Ms. Wicked guessed she was the student who'd brought the boat? Was she the one whose movements the teacher had been tracking? If so, how? And why?

"Oh, that reminds me," said Baby Bear. "Two sisters — members of E.V.I.L. — reported seeing a girl head off in a boat for the island this afternoon."

"And you're just now reporting it?" said Mama Bear.

Goldie sucked in her breath. Those figures she thought she'd glimpsed in the tower window must have been Malorette and Odette. They had to be the sisters the bear meant. And they'd ratted her out. Those . . . rats!

"I am surrounded by nincompoops," groaned Ms. Wicked. Her voice was close now. Right outside the bedroom! "If you'd been quicker about alerting us, maybe your precious chair would still be intact." *Click. Click. Click.* "What's this?" she said suddenly. And then she exclaimed, "Ow! It's that awful hairpin."

Huh? Goldie reached up to pat her hair, but her special hairpin — which might even be her magic charm — was gone. It must have fallen out of her hair before she came into the bedroom! And, ha-ha, it had shocked Ms. Wicked. Again.

"I've seen this pin before," Ms. Wicked said. "It's *hers*. That Goldie girl." Then to one of the bears, she said, "Fetch a wooden spoon to pick it up with, please. Then put it in this little pouch and hand it to me."

A moment later, there was a scraping sound and then Mama Bear's voice said, "Here."

"Let's check the bed*rrr*oom," suggested Papa Bear. "If she's in here, that's the only other place she could be."

Goldie froze beneath the small bed, holding her breath as the bedroom door opened. She heard the bears pad into the room and the *click, click, click* of Ms. Wicked's high heels on the wooden floor. From under the bed, she could see the bears' clawed feet and Ms. Wicked's pointy-toed shoes.

"Nope," said Mama Bear.

"Not he*rrr*e," said Papa Bear.

"Empty," said Baby Bear.

"Don't be idiots," Ms. Wicked snarled. "What kind of guards are you, anyway? Search the room. She's still carrying the tracking device, and it indicates she's in here. She must be hiding!"

Tracking device? What tracking device? Hardly daring to breathe, Goldie listened to the creak of wardrobe doors swinging open and drawers sliding out. "Nothing he*rrr*e," reported Papa Bear in his low, growly voice.

More wardrobe doors opened and more drawers slid out. "Not here, either," said Mama Bear.

"There's nowhere else she could hide," said Baby Bear, "unless . . ." Suddenly, the hem of the bedspread lifted and the smallest bear, who was crouched on the floor, peered into Goldie's eyes. "She's here!" he squeaked in surprise. "It's her! The girl who ate my porridge!"

Here we go again, she thought.

12

Trapped!

"Goldilocks! Come out from under there right this min-ute," Ms. Wicked commanded.

Trapped, Goldie had no choice. She wriggled out from under the bed. "I–I'm sorry," she spluttered as she got to her feet. She clutched her shoes to her chest, one in each hand. Her mind raced to come up with a believable excuse for being inside the cottage. Or on Heart Island, for that matter.

"Why did you have to eat *my* food?" Baby Bear asked peevishly.

Goldie started to explain, but Ms. Wicked interrupted. "Your porridge is not what's important here, you twit," the evil teacher-principal said, pushing Baby Bear aside. Glaring at Goldie, Ms. Wicked tapped the pointy toe of one high-heeled foot impatiently. "Explain yourself!" she demanded.

Goldie's aunt had often barked the same order when she'd caught Goldie doing something she didn't like (which was often), so Goldie had grown adept at coming up with excuses to get herself off the hook for various offenses. But right now, she was stumped.

"Well?" said Ms. Wicked when she didn't reply immediately.

Yikes. She'd better come up with something fast if she didn't want to wind up in the Academy dungeon! Finally, a good story popped into her head. She launched into it. "It's like this. I heard a rumor about a group plotting against E.V.I.L. The group was called . . . um . . . *Against E.V.I.L.*"

Ms. Wicked arched an eyebrow. "Against E.V.I.L.," she repeated. Did she believe the fib? Goldie couldn't tell, but the three bears certainly looked alarmed.

Goldie nodded. "Or maybe it was called *Anti-E.V.I.L.* Something like that, anyway." Before Ms. Wicked could ask her about the source of the rumor, she rushed on. "I also heard that the Society had a meetinghouse on Heart Island and that the *Just Say No to E.V.I.L.* group knew that and was coming out here to spy. So, hoping to be of service to E.V.I.L., I decided to investigate the rumors."

Ms. Wicked cocked her head. "Is that so?" she said, sounding somewhat skeptical. "Nice of you to make a stab at tidying up the dishes while you were investigating, though you did break a chair in the process."

Goldie spread her arms wide in what she hoped was an

open and innocent gesture. "I'm a bit of a clean freak, I guess. And I know it sounds kind of crazy. I didn't believe the rumors at first, either. But then I saw this cottage —"

"Which was locked," Ms. Wicked interrupted her. "Just like Ms. Goose's safe." She shook the hairpin from the pouch she was holding so that it fell onto the bed Goldie had been hiding under. "I've read your tale. Putting two and two together, I figured out that you must have a talent for opening locks. I gather you used *this* to pick both the safe and the cottage door locks?" she said, motioning toward the pin.

"Well, yes," Goldie admitted, unsure where this was going.

To her surprise, Ms. Wicked actually laughed. "Lock picking. Now that's a skill the E.V.I.L. Society could put to use," she said. And this time she definitely sounded amused.

"Awesome! Can I have my hairpin back?" Goldie felt bold enough to ask. She made a move for her pin, but when Baby Bear blocked her, she rambled on. "I didn't realize I'd lost it till I heard voices at the door a few minutes ago and had to find a place to hide. I wasn't sure who it would be." Sudden inspiration struck. "In fact, it might've been those *Down With E.V.I.L.* organizers. Naturally, I thought it could be a good opportunity to spy on them, on E.V.I.L.'s behalf."

"Oh, naturally," said Ms. Wicked. She motioned to Papa Bear to use the spoon again to scoop up the pin and put it back in the pouch she held. But before he could move, the pin surprised everyone by leaping from the bed and sliding itself back into Goldie's hair.

"Well, well. Besides being useful for picking locks, that pin of yours appears to have some magic in it," Ms. Wicked observed. "What else can it do besides leap into your hair and shock others who try to take it?"

"Honestly, I don't know," Goldie admitted with a shrug. She started sidling toward the door.

"But you did use it to unlock Ms. Goose's safe?"

Goldie nodded.

"Only the four keys I asked you to get weren't inside?" Ms. Wicked asked casually.

"Four? But there were only —" Goldie began.

When Ms. Wicked smiled coldly, she realized her mistake. Ms. Wicked had never told her what was inside the safe. And the only way she could have known that four keys was incorrect was if she had actually *seen* the ring of keys. Caught in a lie, Goldie made a break for the door.

"Seize her!" Ms. Wicked shouted to the bears.

Baby Bear nabbed Goldie, but he came away only with her cloak. When she whirled around and snatched it back, Ms. Wicked's sharp eyes fastened on it. "What's that?" she demanded.

Goldie looked down to see that the top of Principal R's tall hat had worked its way out of her cloak pocket in the struggle. "I . . . um . . . I found it under the bed," she said truthfully. Then she added a fib. "Thought it might keep my ears warm on the boat ride back to the Academy. So I'll just be going . . ."

Lickety-split, the bears surrounded her. As they held on to Goldie's arms, Ms. Wicked darted forward and snatched the hat, blanching when she saw whose it was. "You fools!" she exclaimed, shaking the hat at the bears. "How could you have missed seeing this under that bed? If this magic cha . . . I mean *hat* had fallen into the wrong hands." She broke off to glance at Goldie. "Like hers."

"Who, me?" said Goldie. She wriggled against her captors, eyeing the door.

"Here's the thing," Ms. Wicked told her frostily. "You're not nearly as good a liar as you think you are. You obviously lied about the safe being empty. And there is no *Against E.V.I.L.* Or *Anti-E.V.I.L. Society* or whatever. If there were, I'd know about it, believe me."

"Yeah, those little ma*rrr*ble t*rrr*acking devices of hers would have —" Papa Bear began.

"Shut up, you blab*bear*mouth!" Ms. Wicked commanded. Then she whirled on Goldie again. "Besides, that pin of yours is clearly a magic charm. And magic charms only come to those who are good of heart." She said this last with a sneer, as if being "good of heart" was a character defect.

Seeing that the jig was up, Goldie blurted out, "What have you done with Principal R? He was here at the cottage. I know he was!"

For a second, Ms. Wicked looked startled. Then she laughed. "So you were lying about that, too," she said, holding up the crumpled hat. "You knew this was Rumpelstiltskin's hat all along."

Goldie and the three bears gasped when she said his name, but though Goldie thought she heard the wind pick up outside and rustle the trees, nothing else happened. Sadly, the true and rightful principal of Grimm Academy wasn't around to throw his usual tantrum.

Ms. Wicked reshaped the hat with her perfectly manicured fingers so that it was no longer crumpled. "Unfortunately for you," she said to Goldie, "with the hat in my possession, you have no proof of anything. And this hat will be of great use to me, for it has its own sort of magic, which I *will* learn to control. But yes, your former principal was a *guest* here for a few days."

"Where is he now?" Goldie repeated. If only the bears weren't between her and the door, she might be able to escape and . . . and then what? She wasn't at all sure she could outrun them.

"According to the tracker message marble I hid in his boot heel, he's right where we put him. Someplace safe, where busybodies like you are unlikely to discover him," Ms. Wicked replied. Her hard eyes regarded Goldie. "The question now is, what shall we do about you, hmm?"

"*Me?*" Goldie croaked. Until this moment, it hadn't occurred to her that Ms. Wicked might do something really awful to her. Such as take her prisoner and hide her away like poor Principal R. No! She wouldn't let that happen! Thinking fast, she let herself go limp. Baby Bear stumbled under her weight and she twisted away. Startled, the other two bears also let go of her. She grabbed the principal's hat right out of Ms. Wicked's hands and took off running!

Ms. Wicked gasped with outrage. "Stop her, you dimwits!" she yelled. The bears leaped to do her bidding and were soon hot on Goldie's trail. In mere seconds, they had her surrounded in the yard outside.

"Hand over the hat," Ms. Wicked commanded, coming to join them.

"No!" yelled Goldie, cramming it back into the pocket of her cloak instead. At the same time, she felt something long and thin and solid still inside that very pocket. The wand

Prince Foulsmell had given her! With so much going on, she'd forgotten she still had it.

Eyes blazing, Ms. Wicked advanced on her, reaching out. The bears hung back, making way. Just before Ms. Wicked could snatch at the hat, Goldie's hairpin slid from her hair, flew through the air, and pricked Ms. Wicked's hand, shocking her again. *Zzzpt!*

"Ow!" screeched the teacher, drawing back. "Why, you little brat! You and your magic charm will pay for that!"

"Not if I can help it," Goldie shouted. As her hairpin slid itself back in her hair again, she quickly pulled the wand from her pocket and cast a protective bubble around herself. Leaning forward, she rolled and bounced off through the grove.

The last thing she saw as she left the clearing was Ms. Wicked cradling her hurt hand while yelling at the bears. "Get her, you fools! Do you expect me to run in these high heels?"

After a moment's confusion, the bears took off after Goldie. Now and then, they caught up to her and pounced on the bubble, but each time, they bounced off it again and were flung away. *Oof! Oof! Oof!* Eventually, all three wound up flat on their backs on the ground, breathing hard and watching her and her bubble roll off toward the river.

Goldie bounced onward, all the way across Heart Island, going far faster than she could ever have run. As she got closer to the river, she saw Foulsmell arrive and pull his boat up to the dock again. He must have gotten worried and returned for her.

Her momentum propelled her straight toward him. But she couldn't stop! They hadn't learned how to put on the brakes! She saw his surprised face as her bubble hit the side of his boat and bounced high into the air. "Sorry!" she yelled.

Splash! Her bubble hit the water, and she found herself being gently rocked and rolled across the river, all the way back to the Academy. At last, Goldie's bouncing bubble came to a halt on top of GA's dock. She tapped the tip of her wand to the ceiling of her bubble to make it disappear. When it did, she tumbled to the dock.

Glancing back over her shoulder, she could just make out the figures of Ms. Wicked and the three bear guards standing on the other side of the river on Heart Island's shore. They were shaking their fists (and paws) in the air. And for some reason, they were all spinning. No, that was just her dizziness, from all the bouncing. It wasn't long before everything righted, though.

Staring across the river again, she saw that Ms. Wicked's boat was gone. Foulsmell had taken it! Already, he was halfway across the river, paddling toward her and the Academy with Ms. Wicked's boat in tow behind his own.

Jumping to her feet, Goldie pulled the treacherous message marble tracker from her pocket and tossed it as far as she could into the river. "There. Let's see you track me now!" she yelled at Ms. Wicked, even though she probably couldn't hear.

"Look! She's back! And safe!" she heard Polly shout. Goldie turned to see a group of girls that included Rapunzel, Red, Snow, Cinda, Polly, and Briar Rose running toward her from the Pink Castle drawbridge.

Pulling Principal R's hat from her pocket, she waved it in the air. "I found Principal R's hat! The E.V.I.L. Society was hiding him on Heart Island!" she shouted to them.

There were murmurs of shock and anger from the group as they gathered around her. Polly gave her a hug. "I'm so glad you're back. We've been worried about you. Especially when you didn't show up at dinner."

"Foulsmell told us you guys practiced the bubble protection spell —" Rapunzel said to Goldie.

"And it looked like you mastered it," Red interrupted, grinning.

"Good thing," Goldie told her, "or I might not have escaped Ms. Wicked's evil clutches." Then she explained to the other girls all that had happened after Foulsmell had left the island and she'd gone back to retrieve her cloak.

"I can't believe you did something so dangerous," Briar Rose said in a slightly scolding tone after Goldie had finished.

"Are you kidding?" teased Goldie. She laughed. "I can't believe you're saying that. You're the one with the reputation as a daredevil." *Oops!* Had she just fallen back into her old ways of speaking without thinking? Immediately, she worried she'd offended Rose.

But Rose just shrugged. "True, but knight training has tempered my daredevil nature with some much-needed caution."

She looked kind of proud of this fact, Goldie noticed. Was it possible she could somehow temper her own blurt-outs simply by using a little more caution?

Quickly, she explained about the message marble tracker and how Ms. Wicked had said there were more of them around the school. Then she added ruefully, "I only wish I'd found Principal R and not just his hat in the bear guards' cottage. Ms. Wicked admitted they'd been keeping him there. Only, now they've moved him somewhere else!"

"Yeah, but this is a first big step toward finding him," said Snow.

"But I won't be able to spy on the group," Goldie said, frowning. "I've blown my cover completely to bits! And who knows what Ms. Wicked will do to me once she finally gets off the island. At the very least, I'll probably get expelled and have to go back home to live with my aunt." It didn't seem fair, especially now that she was finally starting to make some friends. Not the evil kind, either. She didn't *want* to leave!

Cinda gave her a hug. "We won't let that happen."

"Yeah, we're all in this together," Polly chimed in.

Rapunzel smiled at Goldie. "When we show Principal R's hat to the School Board and tell them where you found it and what Ms. Wicked said, her goose will be cooked!"

"I hope you're right," said Goldie. But she wasn't so sure. Ms. Wicked was a crafty enemy. And she probably told much better lies than any of them ever could, too. What if she was able to convince the helmet-head School Board that she was innocent? Maybe she'd even try to pin the blame for Principal R's disappearance on Goldie somehow. Just thinking about it made her shudder.

"Hey!" called a voice. They looked around to see that Foulsmell had pulled up in his boat.

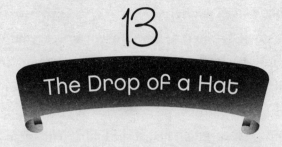

13

The Drop of a Hat

Once inside the entrance to Pink Castle, Goldie and the other students hurriedly agreed among themselves that Rapunzel, Polly, and Foulsmell would accompany Goldie to the Great Hall. The four of them would show Principal R's hat to the five shiny iron helmet-heads that comprised the School Board, and explain what had happened out on Heart Island.

"And you'll report back on the School Board's response right away?" Red asked after everyone had wished Goldie and her companions good luck.

"We will," Goldie promised. As the other students started upstairs to the dorms, she, Foulsmell, Rapunzel, and Polly raced down the first-floor hall together, heading for the Great Hall. The School Board needed to hear their story before Ms. Wicked and the three bears could find a way off the island and catch up to them! "Hey. Where are all the guards?" Goldie asked along the way. "I haven't seen a single one since I got here."

Foulsmell grinned at her. "Forgot to tell you. Word is that there was a disagreement during that meeting with Ms. Wicked this afternoon. Apparently the animals got tired of her yelling at them and telling them what lousy guards they were. Plus, I heard she hadn't paid them, either."

Rapunzel nodded. "And so after the meeting, they all walked off the job. All except the bears, I guess."

"Yeah, too bad they didn't quit, too," said Goldie. "I might have been spared that whole scene on Heart Island!"

Polly and the others chuckled.

Remembering how Ms. Wicked had called the three bears dimwits and fools and worse, Goldie didn't doubt that the first rumor was true. And since the legendary Straw of Gold had yet to produce a fortune, and all attempts to spin it had stopped, Ms. Wicked probably didn't *have* money to pay the guards.

"I wonder where they all went? The guards, I mean," Goldie mused.

"Into Neverwood Forest," Polly replied. "Cinda saw the zebras and foxes and all the rest heading that way."

By now, they'd reached the enormous, ornate doors to the Great Hall. Foulsmell looked over at Goldie. "Ready?" he asked.

A ripple of nervousness ran down her spine, but she squared her shoulders and stood straighter. "Ready," she said.

But before they could make a move to go in, the doors were flung open toward them from the inside. Goldie froze in horror as Ms. Wicked came barreling out. She smirked when their eyes met. "Why so surprised? Didn't expect me to show up so soon?" she hissed. "Well, never underestimate me. I have other ways to travel that don't involve boats."

"By broomstick, you mean?" Goldie joked.

"Or by mirror?" Rapunzel put in. Goldie remembered that the long-haired goth girl had been locked in a tower with Ms. Wicked and other E.V.I.L. Society members not long ago and had later reported that members were able to go from place to place by popping in and out of mirrors. Maybe that's how she'd really gotten off the island.

Ms. Wicked wasn't telling, though.

"Where are those bear guards, hmm? Did they quit perhaps? Like the rest of your guards?" asked Foulsmell.

He must have guessed correctly since Ms. Wicked grimaced. Ignoring his questions, she cocked her head toward the far end of the Great Hall, where the School Board sat on their shelf above the east balcony. "Tell them whatever you want," she said with a smirk. "It won't do any of you a bit of good."

Then her eyes narrowed and she took a step toward Goldie, whispering, "Mark my words, Goldilocks, your days here are numbered!"

But Ms. Wicked jumped back in alarm when Goldie's pearl-flower hairpin slid from her hair to hover directly in front of the would-be principal. It buzzed there in midair like some kind of pretty, but dangerous, stinging wasp. Dangerous to *some* people, anyway. The evil kind.

A flicker of fear passed over the teacher's face. Then, without another word, she scurried on down the hall. *Click! Click! Click!*

Its job done for the time being, the hairpin slid back into Goldie's hair. "Magic charm," she explained when the other three students looked at her in astonishment. "Ms. Wicked told me so back on Heart Island. Apparently, part of its magic is that it *sticks* up for me."

"Come forward, scholars!" the five helmet-heads chorused now. Goldie gulped. Whatever she told them, it would be her word against Ms. Wicked's. And since Ms. Wicked was a teacher, the acting principal, and a persuasive liar, what chance was there that the School Board would believe what she, a mere student, had to say?

With a sinking heart, she took a step toward the end of the Hall. She was glad, at least, for the company of her friends. Rapunzel and Polly linked arms with her for sup-port, and Foulsmell, who was right behind them, murmured words of encouragement. "Don't worry. We have your back."

Before Goldie could reply, the four of them came to a stop below the balcony shelf. The middle head, which had a red feather sticking up from the top of its helmet, spoke to them first. "We have just heard from Ms. Wicked about the disturbing events of this evening. Which one of you is Goldilocks?" it asked, its visor clacking open and shut as it spoke.

Goldie's throat seized up. For a moment, she couldn't speak, but then Rapunzel and Polly gave her hands gen-tle squeezes, which helped to calm her. "Me. *I* am," she admitted.

"You stand accused of breaking and entering a cottage with intent to steal, acts of vandalism, and falsely plant-ing evidence to destroy a teacher's reputation," said the helmet-head to the left of the middle one. It had a yellow feather sticking out of the top of its helmet. "Do you wish to respond to these accusations?"

"What! That's preposterous. Um, I mean yes, I do want to respond. It's true that I did break into the bear guards' cottage," she confessed. "But only because I was trying to find Principal R, not because I intended to steal."

"And what made you think he would be there?" asked another of the helmet-heads. This one had a blue feather sticking out the top of its helmet.

She considered the question. "Rumors and a gut feeling, I guess," she replied at last.

"Rumors? *Gut* feeling?" repeated the yellow-feathered helmet-head. Its tone of voice made it sound like those were very weak reasons for breaking into the cottage. Especially the gut feeling part, she realized. After all, these helmets didn't even have guts to get feelings *in*!

"Maybe those seem like kind of lame reasons to you, but if I hadn't acted on them, I wouldn't have found this." With a feeling of excitement, she whipped out Principal R's hat to show them. Seeing it caused a ripple of clanking and murmurs among the five School Board members.

"Oh, so you *did* steal something!" exclaimed the helmet-head farthest to her right. It had a green feather on its helmet.

"No! I mean yes, I did take it," she said, feeling flustered. "But only as evidence that Principal R had been in the cottage! After I found it under one of the beds there, Ms. Wicked pretty much admitted that she and her bear guards had imprisoned him on Heart Island, then moved him somewhere else."

Goldie also remembered that the teacher had very nearly called the principal's hat a magic *charm*. Could grown-ups even *have* a magic charm? If Principal R was good of heart (which Goldie was convinced he was) despite his tantrums, why not?

"Hmm," said the yellow-feathered helmet-head. "But how do we know that's really Principal R's hat?"

"Know anyone else here at the Academy who wears a hat like that?" Foulsmell blurted from behind Goldie. He sounded exasperated.

At his outburst, the School Board murmured among themselves for a few moments, their visors softly creaking.

"It *looks* like his hat," the middle, red-feathered helmet-head conceded at last. He seemed to be the one in charge, so Goldie wondered if maybe he was the *head* helmet-head. "But how do we know you didn't find the hat somewhere else and plant it in the cottage to incriminate Ms. Wicked?"

"Is that what she told you?" Rapunzel exclaimed, her dark eyes flashing. "Ms. Wicked *would* say that. She and E.V.I.L. want to take control of the Academy!"

"Yeah," Polly chimed in. "And since you've all made her the acting principal, she's halfway to her goal!"

That last might have been a slight exaggeration, but Goldie appreciated her friends' spirited defense of her. Now there was even more murmuring and clacking of visors among the School Board members.

"Thank you for coming," the red-feathered helmet-head said at last. "We've heard all we need to hear for now."

Goldie couldn't believe she and her friends were being dismissed already. "What? So that's it?" she blurted. Heat rose in her cheeks. "What happens next? Is anyone going to go looking for Principal R?"

She took a step forward and craned her neck to look up at the helmet-heads. "And what are you going to do about Ms. Wicked?" she asked, her voice rising. "She told me my days here are numbered. Is she allowed to threaten me like that? Expel me, even?"

"Calm yourself, scholar!" rebuked the middle helmet-head. "Principal R's disappearance is being investigated. As will your accusations against Principal Wicked."

Goldie opened her mouth again to protest, but Rapunzel beat her to it. "But Ms. Wicked is evil! You can't let her —"

"Silence!" shouted the red-feathered helmet-head. Then in a quieter voice, it added, "No one will be expelled. Now please go. Return to your rooms. Study. Academy life will go on."

As Goldie and her friends turned to trudge back the way they'd come, the yellow-feathered helmet-head called after them, "Don't forget. The brothers Grimm intended

Grimmlandia to be a safe haven for *all* fairy-tale and nursery rhyme characters, regardless of their literary roles. No one can be banished merely for being evil. No more than they can for being good."

Yes, thought Goldie. But even so, surely the brothers Grimm wouldn't have tolerated Ms. Wicked's and E.V.I.L.'s actions. Because those actions threatened not just individual students like her, and not just GA, but the entire realm of Grimmlandia.

"Investigation, inschmestigation," Foulsmell grumbled with uncharacteristic derision as the four of them made their way from the Hall. He cocked a thumb back toward the School Board. "I wouldn't trust those bucket heads to know how to conduct an investigation as far as I could catapult them! For one thing, they're all stuck to a board!"

"Too true," said Rapunzel, grinning.

"But what can we do about it?" Polly asked plaintively.

"If only Principal R were here. He'd soon set things straight," Goldie said. She was about to stuff his hat, which might even be his magic charm, back inside her pocket, when she remembered what she'd read in the *All About Magic Charms* booklet in the Grimm brothers' room. That a bond with a magic charm could never be broken. That if you were ever separated from your charm, it could return you to a place of safety. Why hadn't Principal

R tried to return himself to his hat charm before now, though?

Was it possible the magic charm itself had to be in a place of safety for you to return to it? she wondered. Goldie stopped in her tracks. The bear's cottage was definitely not a place of safety. But the Great Hall was.

"Wait," she said to the others, her excitement rising again. She wasn't sure if what she was about to do would succeed, but she had to try.

Holding the hat high in one hand, she spoke to it. "Principal Rumpelstiltskin needs you. Can you please return him here, to this place of safety?" Then she let go of the hat. When it immediately dropped to the floor, her heart plunged with it.

They all stood there, staring from the hat to her and back again. And then, suddenly, the hat stirred. It gave a flutter. Then did a spin. Finally, it lifted again under its own power and began to whirl around in circles like a little black tornado. It spun so fast Goldie and the others felt dizzy just watching it. Then something appeared whirling underneath it. A figure maybe three feet tall at most.

"Principal R!" Goldie and her friends shouted out as he and his hat slowed and finally stopped spinning. The principal was so dizzy, he tumbled to the stone floor.

"Dagnabbit!" he shouted as he picked himself up, dusted off his hat, and stuck it on top of his head again. He looked around. "Where is she? When I get my hands on Ms. Wicked, I'll, I'll . . ."

"All hail the great and goodly principal of Grimm Academy!" the School Board chorused from the end of the Great Hall, visors clanking. The colored feathers at the top of their helmets snapped to attention, standing up straighter than ever.

"Never mind all that!" Principal R growled at them. "Time's a-wastin'. Where's Ms. Wicked?"

The helmet-heads' visors clinked and clanked, but none of them seemed to have a clue.

"I'd say they were tongue-tied, if they *had* tongues to tie," Foulsmell quipped and Goldie smiled at his jest.

"She was just here," Rapunzel told the principal. "But she took off when we arrived with your hat, which Goldie found in the three bears' cottage."

"Ms. Wicked falsely accused her of planting your hat there to incriminate her," Polly added indignantly.

A storm cloud passed over Principal Rumpelstiltskin's face. Was he about to have another of his famed tantrums? Goldie wondered, taking a careful step back. "I bet she went up to her . . . er . . . *your* office," she said. "She took it over after you disappeared."

"She did WHAT?" shouted the principal. The knuckles on his clenched fists went white with fury. He twisted his head to glare at the School Board. "You hollow-headed tin cans!" he yelled. "She principal-napped me! And then she pushed you into appointing her in my place after she and E.V.I.L. changed my fairy tale to make me look incompetent, I bet! I got a load of their so-called 'improvements' in my fairy tale. Baby Bear made me read him to sleep with it each night while I was locked in that cottage on Heart Island. What a bunch of baloney."

The School Board's visors clinked and clanked in dismay and their feathers drooped in shame. Before they could speak up, however, Principal R swept them with a final look of disgust and then stormed from the Hall.

"Come along!" he called over his shoulder to Goldie and her friends. "We're going to set things straight!"

"Have a happily-ever-after evening!" the School Board chorused pathetically as Principal R, Goldie, Foulsmell, Rapunzel, and Polly left the Hall together and raced up the grand staircase to the fourth floor.

"Principal R! You're back!" Ms. Jabberwocky called out happily when he burst through the outer office door and headed for his old office. "You don't know how tulgey glad I am to see you!"

Goldie wondered why the dragon-lady assistant was still working in the office, since she'd heard the Hickory Dickory Dock clock bong eight times on the way up the stairs. But then she noticed what Ms. Jabberwocky was doing. Creating signs that listed even harsher school rules that Ms. Wicked must've made up while the rest of them stood before the School Board. One sign read: VISITS TO THE ISLANDS ARE STRICTLY PROHIBITED.

Obviously happy to see her, too, the principal smiled at Ms. Jabberwocky before putting a finger to his lips. Catching on right away, Ms. Jabberwocky clamped her toothy jaws shut. With a swish of her dragon tail, she knocked the stack of rule signs she'd made into the trash bin. Then she waved a sharp-clawed hand toward the door beyond her desk. "She's in there," she whispered.

They all watched as Principal R approached his old office. His neck and face turned a deep red when he saw the new brass plate on the door. "Principal Wicked, my foot!" he hissed. Unable to restrain his temper any longer, he burst through the door. Goldie and the others were right behind him. And so was Ms. Jabberwocky. "The jig is up!" he boomed out.

Ms. Wicked was sitting on the gold throne behind Principal R's desk, refreshing her lipgloss, as everyone entered. At the sight of the principal, she paled in alarm. A flicker of fear passed over her face, but she quickly regained her composure. Sneering at him, she rose from his throne. "So you escaped, did you?" she said, walking around the desk. Carelessly, she glided over to drop her lipgloss in her handbag, which sat on the antique table where she'd once interviewed Goldie. "I wonder how you managed that?"

"His hat brought him back," Goldie stated flatly. "Thanks for letting me know that it was his magic charm, by the way."

Ms. Wicked gazed at her through narrowed eyes. "Smart girl. Too smart for your own good. I was afraid you might figure that out. I didn't mean to let it slip that —"

Foulsmell's dark eyes flashed. "Which only means you're not as clever as you think you are."

Ms. Wicked looped the handles of her handbag over one arm. Then she reached up to pat her hair, moving to stare into one of the many mirrors she'd hung on the wall. "You're wrong," she said. "I'm cleverer than all of the *good* students at this Academy put together. Don't believe me? Watch this!"

Before anyone could react to stop her, she leaped into the mirror and disappeared, handbag, high heels, and all.

"Dadgummit and blast her pointy shoes!" Principal R yelled, hopping up and down like a cricket. Then he threw himself onto the floor and began to flail his arms and legs in the air.

Goldie and the others watched in amazement, and some amusement as well. Ms. Wicked was deviously good at hiding her true feelings behind that frozen smile of hers, but you always knew how Principal R felt about things because he let it all hang out. It was good to have him back.

"Bandersnatch! Come along, grimmble students," Ms. Jabberwocky said, shepherding them out of the room. She was grinning wider than Goldie had ever seen her grin, obviously as delighted as they were to have their true principal back.

Out in the fourth-floor hallway again, Polly asked the others, "Think Ms. Wicked is gone forever?"

"Doubtful," said Rapunzel as they stood around to talk for a moment. "But we can always hope."

Goldie nodded. "It would be nice to think we've seen the last of her, but —"

"— seems unlikely," Foulsmell finished. "Not with the rest of E.V.I.L. still in operation."

"I wish we could get organized somehow to better fight them," said Polly.

Rapunzel nodded.

"Hey! You know what? Maybe we can," said Goldie. She twisted one of her curly golden locks around a finger. "I told Ms. Wicked and the bears a whopper of a lie when they trapped me in the cottage. I told them I'd heard a rumor about a group plotting against E.V.I.L. And that it was called Against E.V.I.L. or Anti-E.V.I.L. She didn't buy it. But no matter. Now I'm thinking . . . why not get organized and start a group like that for real?"

There was a pause as her suggestion sank into everyone's brains.

Then Rapunzel announced, "I like it! I mean, for a long time, E.V.I.L.'s existence was a secret. But now everyone knows about them. Those of us who've been trying to investigate on our own could use more support from one another. *And* protection! One formal group with formal meetings might be just what we all need."

"I'm in," said Foulsmell. "And I know some of my other friends will want to join."

Polly nodded. "Me too. But before we ask around, which name should we tell everyone? We might sound more organized if the group already has one." The four of them had begun to take a few steps toward the grand staircase, but now they paused, wanting to decide the matter before talking to the others who were waiting for them in the upstairs dorms.

"We could pick from the ones Goldie came up with," said Rapunzel. "Like Against E.V.I.L.?"

"Hmm," said Goldie. "But now that I think about it, maybe our group name should stand *for* something instead of *against*?"

"I know!" Polly exclaimed. "How about G.O.O.D.? Get it? As in the *opposite* of E.V.I.L.?"

Foulsmell nodded. "E.V.I.L. stands for Exceptional Villains in Literature. So what would each letter in G.O.O.D. stand for?"

"*G* for Good. And then something something something?" Polly said uncertainly.

"But not all of us who wanted to find Principal R and don't like what Ms. Wicked and E.V.I.L. are doing are necessarily 'good' characters in the rhymes and tales," Rapunzel reminded her. "Take Wolfgang, for instance."

Or, to be totally truthful, me, mused Goldie. She thought for a few seconds, then looked at Polly. "Having the *G* stand for Good was a *G*-for-Great-idea, but maybe that's too much of a *good* thing," she said carefully. "Maybe we could keep the acronym G.O.O.D., but the *G* in it could stand for *Grimm*."

Foulsmell piped up, saying, "Yeah! What if, taken together, the letters in G.O.O.D. stand for Grimm Organization of Defense?"

Polly clapped her hands together, not looking at all like she'd suffered a put-down or been hurt that Goldie and the others hadn't loved her idea. "Tea-rrific!" she proclaimed. Everyone laughed at her pun.

And Goldie smiled, too, thinking that she'd surprised even herself by not blurting out something hurtful to trample on Polly's idea, which was the kind of thing she might have unwittingly done in the past. If only the library gooseknob could have heard her! Because maybe she'd learned something in the past few days about thinking before you speak. She'd managed to express her disagreement, yet leave Polly smiling and their friendship intact.

"I like it!" she said. "It'll define our group's aim — to defend Grimmlandia from all kinds of threats, whether from E.V.I.L. or the Nothingterror or whatever!"

Rapunzel nodded. "And membership won't be limited to so-called *good* literary figures. All who pledge to defend Grimmlandia and the Academy — including villainous characters with at least halfway-good hearts — can become members of G.O.O.D."

"Sounds G.O.O.D.," Foulsmell said with a grin. As they neared the staircase he split off from the girls to head in the direction of Gray Castle to talk to his guy friends.

"Bye," the girls chorused.

"C'mon, let's go tell the rest of our friends," Rapunzel said to Goldie and Polly.

Our friends! she'd said. Meaning friends of hers, Polly's, and Goldie's. She'd said it so casually, but her words made Goldie's heart sing. Because it was true. She'd actually made some friends here at GA. Friends who accepted and valued her for who she was regardless of her fairy-tale role.

As Rapunzel and Polly started upstairs, Goldie held back a moment. "I'll catch up," she told them.

Then she called to Foulsmell who was heading back down the hall to the staircase that led up to the Gray Castle dorms. "Wait!" she said, jogging after him. "I never did properly apologize for the whole puppy thing with Malorette and Odette," she told him once she reached his side.

He looked away, shrugging a little uncomfortably. "That's okay, I —"

"No, it's not okay," she interrupted, leaning around to catch his eye again. "I'm *really*, *really* sorry. I hated how they acted and should have said something right then. I just thought my bubble protection practice coach should know that," she said. "Without your help and the wand you brought, I might have wound up bear breakfast today."

Foulsmell shrugged again, but now he looked pleased. "Sure, no problem."

She smiled at him. "So I'll return the wand tomorrow in class. But are we buds from now on? Good ones?"

He blushed bright red, looking really flattered. "Definitely." Just then, a couple of his friends, Prince Awesome and Prince Prince, appeared at the end of the hall, calling his name.

"Just a sec!" Foulsmell called back. Turning to go, he bid her farewell. "Later, then." He headed off, but then stopped after a few steps and called back to her, "Hey, I hope Mistress Hagscorch is making her Hurraying Hero Sandwiches for lunch tomorrow. Because you've earned one!" With that, he turned and loped off toward his friends.

A warm feeling spread through Goldie as she watched him go. *Foulsmell thought she was a hero!* Though it was really the magic charm *hat* that had brought the principal back, she valued Foulsmell's opinion and hugged his approval close. Unlike some of the other princes at GA, she decided, he was not too grand, not too ordinary, but in fact . . . just right. At least in her opinion.

She pushed back her golden locks and her hand brushed her hairpin charm. It had played an important role in her escape from Ms. Wicked and the bears, too, of course. *What other magic can it do?* she wondered. Time would tell.

For now, she was eager, with Rapunzel and Polly's help, to tell the girls waiting for them all that had happened today. About how Ms. Wicked was gone — at least for a while — and how Principal R was back . . . for G.O.O.D. She smiled at her own pun. While thinking about plans for their new society, she skipped the rest of the way down the hall. Then she raced upstairs to join all her new, amazing, forever, grimmtastic friends!

A Grimmtastic girl named Cinderella is starting her first week at Grimm Academy on the wrong foot. Cinda's totally evil stepsisters are out to make her life miserable. The Steps tease Cinda, give her terrible advice about life at the Academy, and even make her look bad in front of her new friends, Red, Snow, and Rapunzel! But when Cinda overhears the Steps plotting a villainous deed that could ruin Prince Awesome's ball, Cinda, her new friends, and a pair of magical glass slippers have to stop them — before the last stroke of midnight!

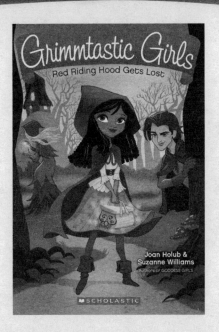

Red Riding Hood is thrilled to try out for the school play. Acting is her dream, and she's great at it — too bad she has stage fright! After a grimmiserable audition, Red decides to focus on helping her friends Cinda, Snow, and Rapunzel save Grimm Academy from the E.V.I.L. Society. But when Red gets lost in Neverwood forest and runs into Wolfgang, who might be part of E.V.I.L., she needs her magic basket and a grimmazingly dramatic performance to figure out what's going on!

No matter how many lucky charms she wears, Snow White can't catch a break. She's especially worried that her step-mom, Ms. Wicked, is a member of the E.V.I.L. Society. Snow and her friends Red, Cinda, and Rapunzel are trying to stop E.V.I.L.'s plans to destroy Grimm Academy, but Snow seems to be jinxing all their efforts. Her luck might change if she can find her own truly magical charm — before it falls into E.V.I.L. hands!

Rapunzel's enchanted, fast-growing hair can be a nuisance, especially when an accident gives it magical powers she can't control! But Rapunzel can't let her grimmorrible hair woes distract her — she and her friends Cinda, Red, and Snow are trying to save Grimm Academy from the E.V.I.L. Society. Once Rapunzel tracks down her magic charm, she won't let a bad hair day get in the way of stopping E.V.I.L.!

Sleeping Beauty — who just goes by her middle name, Rose — has always been a daredevil. But according to her fairy tale, after her twelfth birthday Rose must avoid all sharp objects. That isn't easy at Grimm Academy, where enchanted items can also be dangerous. Rose will have to stay wide awake to keep out of trouble — and to join the fight against E.V.I.L.!